Snatch and Grab:
Was It Really Worth It?

by
Lakiesha "Stoney" Smith

My Loud Publishing
Cleveland, OH

ISBN: 978-0-578-87994-9

Some names herein have been changed to protect the innocent.

Stoney email:
getitgurl247@icloud.com

FB: @lakieshasmith
IG: @myloudradio/inmate2inspiration

Edited by: Alfred Cleveland for CleveCo Studios, LLC

Contents

INTRODUCTION....................i

CHAPTER ONE....................1

CHAPTER TWO....................7

CHAPTER THREE....................13

CHAPTER FOUR....................21

CHAPTER FIVE....................27

CHAPTER SIX....................35

CHAPTER SEVEN....................41

CHAPTER EIGHT....................47

CHAPTER NINE....................53

CHAPTER TEN....................61

CHAPTER ELEVEN....................67

CHAPTER TWELVE....................75

CHAPTER THIRTEEN....................83

CHAPTER FOURTEEN....................87

CHAPTER FIFTEEN....................95

CHAPTER SIXTEEN....................101

I would like to start off by dedicating this book to my father, may he rest in peace. He always knew I had so much potential and I'm sure he's smiling down on me from heaven, so proud of me.

RIP Daddy I love you.

Introduction

I remember it like it was yesterday. The rain was pounding down on my roof so hard it woke me up. I had set my alarm clock for 7 that morning, but clearly it was 6am when I rolled over and looked out the window. The sky looked gloomy. Real gloomy. Something in my gut told me to call my lawyer and get another court-date continuance, but I was just ready to get this shit over and done with so I could go back to living my life. I sat there in my bed a while just thinking how much had changed in my life over the course of a year. Shit was crazy. *Could finally put it all behind me*, I thought, and I couldn't fucking wait.

I hopped out the bed and started getting myself together. My lawyer told me to wear something nice as if I came looking crazy the last time, but I did as he said and spent the whole day before looking for a good court suit. You know them suits that make you look guilty but remorseful?

My mom had stayed the night at my house. She insisted I let her come to court with me. I started to tell her no, but didn't feel like arguing about it. The plan was to get Derek dressed and off to the daycare before the hearing. Oh, where's my manners—Derek is my son, the love of my life who was about to be 2 in two months. Some days I still be tripping I got a kid. Prior to having him I was a wild child, but his lil ass had slowed me all thee way the fuck down. I remember before I had a kid I use to be like "When I have a kid I'm still gon be doing me!" Yeah okay. Lately it seemed like I was doing whatever the fuck Derek wanted to do and I wasn't mad at all.

I finished getting dressed so I could have enough time to make a lil meal before we headed out. I was a breakfast kind of girl. Bitch might not eat for the rest of the day, but sis was gon make sure she started her day with a good meal. As we was driving down the street I was just looking at my lil man in the mirror. He made me so happy man. If I ain't never did shit right before in my life, this would be my first. I literally thanked God every day for him. Having kids really makes you start thinking a whole different way, well, that is for the people who actually wanna be good parents. Some folks be popping out kids and still doing the same shit they been doing forever. Naw, I wanted better for my mine.

I looked at the time and noticed that it was going quicker than I thought, or I was just dragging my ass per usual. I pulled up to the daycare, grabbed Derek, and hurried up into the building. As I was walking out one of his teachers was like, "Good look today girl."

"Thanks boo," I responded, looking back, but said to myself, *Girrllll, why is you all in my business chile.* I really wanted to tell her, *Good luck with that new hairdo*, but whatever. I might have been a little on the edge but I hated when people act like they fake cared. Most of the time they just be nosey as fuck.

I took a deep breath and hopped in the car, heading for the freeway. My plan was to take the street way, but since I was running late Eddy Road freeway it was. I turned my music on trying to get my head in the right place, but of course my mom was like, "Can you please not turn that up so loud? It gives me a headache." I swear this was not the time for her shit. She was blowing my high and I wasn't even high.

As I pulled up to park I wondered why parking always be high as fuck when you go to court? Seems like all these courts want is to take your money and work your damn nerves! On God, after all this shit was over I wanted out this life. Just give me a 9-to-5 and a corny boyfriend and I was good.

I had been so stressed about this case I done got high blood pressure. It was all beginning to be a lil too much. Stepping out the car, I reached in the backseat for my blazer and out of nowhere it just started raining like crazy! I spent the entire morning on my hair and make-up, and now this. Like, you gotta be fucking kidding me! At this point, I had an attitude. I wanted to turn my ass around, go back home, get in the bed and try this out another day but here goes my mother aggy ass: "A little rain ain't never hurt nobody." This coming from somebody with a finger-waved wig on. She was right though. Might as well get it over with today and be done. I grabbed a sweater that was in the back, threw it over my head and ran as quick as I could to the door. Inside the courthouse, I was drenched you hear me? Hair wet, suit wet, feet wet, everything. Ughhh. I should've smoked that blunt like I wanted to cause right now my nerves was shot. I put my shit through the metal detector and headed on up trying to make myself look as decent as I could. The one thing I hated about coming to court was the feeling I got walking through them doors. It was a feeling I could never describe. If you ever been to court, you know.

Everybody knew me to be the strong friend—the one who keeps it all together while everyone else falls apart. That wasn't an easy title to hold either. I never asked to be that, but somehow that's who I was. Every time, and I mean every time I came to court, strong friend turned into a lil vulnerable bitch. Surrounded by bailiffs, prosecutors, lawyers and judges, you really don't feel so strong. I didn't like this shit at all.

Soon as I got off the elevator the first person I saw was my lawyer. Of course, he was on the phone as usual acting like he was Johnny Cochran or some shit. When he saw me he hung up and came over.

"Good morning Ms. Smith. I already talked with the prosecutor and everything should go as planned," he said, looking me in the eye. *Should*, I thought, key word. "I think you are going to walk out of here with 1-3 years probation, tops." *Think*, I thought again. Sounds good right?

Sure, I said to myself. One-to-3 years of probation? Did he not know I was a weed head. I swear this day was getting worst by the second.

"I'm just ready for all this shit to be over with sir." Walking towards the courtroom, I heard my lawyer call my name. Oh, what was I thinking! I had forgot to give this man the last of his lil change I owed him and we wasn't bout to do nathan without him getting his coins. He had charged me $7,000 for my case and I really couldn't complain cause he was a dog for real. I could've got a million other lawyers at a cheaper price, but I really didn't like playing with my freedom like that. This was the best $7,000 I spent in a long time. I gave him the little hoe ass $500 I owed him and kept it moving. How come when you owe somebody some money you get an attitude when you gotta pay them?

The moment I walked in the courtroom I heard the judge tearing somebody's ass up. Butterflies instantly started fluttering in my stomach. Don't you hate when you go to court and some idiot is in there pissing the judge off over some stupid shit? *Look asshole just tell her the truth. You smoke crack, you got high, and you tried to steal a lawnmower out of home depot cause you needed to hit that pipe! Let her send you to treatment so I can get the fuck on sir. Damn!!!!* The judge ended up giving him 20 days or so then told him get his life together.

State of Ohio vs. Lakiesha Smith, was called. Once again that feeling was back. Bitch started breathing all hard trying not to look nervous and scared at the same time. I felt my heart drop to the floor. I was just laughing at the crackheads story 10 seconds ago now all of a sudden I'm feeling like the crackhead.!

"Good morning, Ms. Smith" the judge said.

"Good morning, Your honor," I responded in my most Martha Stewart voice ever. I had one of the meanest judges that worked for the county. When I first told my lawyer who she was he was like, *Oh this gone be a tough one.* I sat there watching her look through my files. I really couldn't see her face so I didn't really know what she was on.

"Ms. Smith it looks like you're no stranger to the system," she said, with her eyes peering over her glasses. I gave that bitch the side eye when she said that. "I'm looking at your record and to me it looks like you take the Judicial system for a joke." I was speechless. The shade in her voice wasn't sitting well with my spirit at all. She continued: "I came in here with every intention on giving you probation, but after further review I think you need to learn a lesson this time around. Ms. Smith, I'm sentencing you to a mandatory 3 years at the Ohio Reformatory for Women."

I couldn't believe this shit! I felt myself getting hot and flustered, but I managed to whisper to my lawyer, "Did she say 3 years? What's the Ohio Reformatory for Women?" He shushed me. I wanted to grab this white mother fucka by his collar and say don't you ever shhh me bitch I paid you 7 thousand, ain't no shushing! But I was trying to remain calm and still understand what was going on.

"You have been given far too many chances throughout the years," she reiterated again, "and today it stops. You will do 3 years in Marysville with 1 year Post-release Control when you get out. Now please use this time to get your act together. Bailiff, take her out my courtroom." My body went numb. I looked back at my mom but I could barely see straight. I started blinking uncontrollably cause I just knew this was a dream, or a nightmare shall I say. I looked over at my lawyer as the bailiff was putting the handcuffs on: "What the fuck John? What the fuck is going on?"

"I'll have you back home in no time Ms. Smith." No time. I think I blacked out at that moment cause the next thing I remember is me waking up in a cell. When I woke up I was sick. No like for real sick to my stomach. I wanted to throw up, but instead I just fell to the floor and cried my damn eyes out. All I could think about was Derek. My little baby boy was only 2 now. We hadn't been apart from each other for more than two days since he was born.

The tears just kept flowing. It hurt so bad. I had never felt a pain like this in my life. It felt like I was dying. My whole body was weak. Three years though? Whatever happened to my high- priced lawyer? That nigga didn't say shit. He just let the judge dog-walk me and didn't even try to save me. The fuck I pay him 7 bands for? I started crying again.

I sat there laying on the floor, tears just rolling down my face wondering how the fuck did my life come to this. How did I get so greedy and sloppy that I ended up on my way to prison. I sat there on the floor in the nasty ass county jail sick to my stomach crying my eyes out. All for what? Some money! Some money done caused me to be taken away from my son. I think I cried all the way until they took me to booking.

I slept that whole day away, just crying and nodding off. Imagine for a moment your only kid being raised by someone other than yourself for three long years. Just thinking about it now makes me feel empty. The CO's had come to my door about three different times asking me if I wanted food, but I couldn't even move. My body was numb. I didn't want anything but to be at home. I could not believe the judge gave me three years for a fucking boosting case. Was she for real? That day I had to cry more than I've ever cried my whole life. I was mad at the judge, mad at my lawyer, mad at the world, but most of all I was mad at myself. Mad at myself, because this wasn't me. I could do better. How did I manage to let my love for money overpower my love for my kid? This was absolutely the worst day of my life! Well, at least I thought it was.

Chapter 1

Allow me to introduce myself. They call me Stoney, and no, I wasn't named after Jada Pinkett's character in *Set It Off*. To be exact, I do think Jada and I was hitting licks at the same time, ha. I was actually named after this guy from the hood. He was a crazy, slick talking, weed smoking cool cat, and I think people thought of him in me so they nicknamed me K-Stoney. I always thought the K made it too hard, so I dropped it and stuck with Stoney.

I'm a midwest girl born and raised in Cleveland, Ohio. East Cleveland to be exact. See you gotta make sure you let people know the difference because East Cleveland people was very different from a lot of folks. We had a certain kinda swag about us and we loved getting money. People don't really know too much about Cleveland except that Bone, Thugs and Harmony and King James from there. Well, he's actually from Akron, but we claim him in Cleveland, you know, since we won that championship in 2016 or whatever.

I don't know what you may have heard about Cleveland, but it's a pretty tough city. Trust me, if you ain't sucking the right niggas dick, or if you ain't cool with the local "celebrities," you was gone have to work *real* hard for whatever you wanted. I always said Cleveland either gone make me or break me. I chose to let it make me.

I was born January 2nd, 1979, yup, almost a New Year's baby so partying was in my blood since birth. I was born to a loving father

We gotta do something to make some money. I sat there for a while and was like, *Let's do a lemonade stand.* My homegirl looked at me crazy cause she probably was thinking how the hell we gon even buy the stuff we needed to get started. I was always that friend coming up with crazy ass ideas that no one else could understand. I was so thirsty for that pickle though, and was determined to make some money to get it!

I went and asked my mom for $2. Of course, she gave me $2 in food stamps. We walked to the store anyway and once we got there I realized, not only did we need lemonade, but we needed sugar, cups, and maybe even ice. I sat there wondering how I was bout to get all that stuff with two lil measly dollars. I told my girl to take the $2 dollars and buy a gallon of already made lemonade. With $2, I wasn't never gon be able to get all that stuff so we was bout to cheat and get the lemonade already made in a bottle. I walked to the back of the store looking bout paranoid as ever. We was in our neighborhood corner store which wasn't big at all. I was walking around looking for some cups and when I found em I opened up the pack and stuffed a whole stack in the sleeve of my coat and walked out. When I met up with my girl, she had the lemonade and to her surprise I had the cups.

"You stole them?" she asked. I'm like, "Yeah. We need to get this money." Her mouth dropped.

"You crazy? What if you got caught?"

"Let's not think about the what ifs. Let's just get ready to go sell these cups of lemonade and make this money friend," and that's exactly what we did. We sat there and sold about 15 cups of lemonade at 50 cents apiece and had enough money to buy not only the pickle, but we had some change left for our pockets. Right then is when I started loving the hustle, and it wasn't just about the money—it was and my mama. I said it like that because I have one of them mamas who's just one of them mamas—know what I mean? She was the kinda person who made sure it was food on the table, but sorta missed out on showing me how to prepare it myself.

I think growing up I probably remember her telling me she loved me like ten times. I'm sure that didn't mean she didn't love me, I just don't think she knew how to show it. That had a lot to do with how she was raised though. You know they say you can't show nobody love if nobody never showed you *how* to love. I got lucky though. For whatever my mom didn't do, my dad picked up the slack. I had one of them dads that over-loved me, if that's possible. I am 100% a full-fledge Daddy's girl. I remember growing up, no matter what was going on throughout the day, he always managed to make sure he called me to tell me he loved me. It could be a blizzard, a national disaster, or just him working late—he still managed to call me before the day was over to tell me that.

Him and my mom separated when I was like two, so we lived in separate homes, but that didn't stop him from coming to see me and talking to me daily. I thank God I had a loving dad, cause babyyyyyy, it could've been ugly if I didn't. So when people tell me I can be sooooooo sweet, yet sooooooo cold at times, I know that's just my mama and my daddy in me.

Growing up in Cleveland made me a hustler by nature. I use to hear people say Cleveland was the Mistake on the Lake, but me being here was no mistake at all. Even as a teenager I had the hustler spirit in me early.

One time when I was 12, I told one of my friends I wanted a pickle from the corner store. Neither of us had a penny to our name. I'm like, more about being in control of what I wanted and not having to wait for somebody else to get it for me. I liked the way money felt in my hands too. Still haven't figured out if that was a gift or a curse.

Growing up, I guess you can say I was broke. Well maybe not broke. My dad had a great job and made sure I had everything I needed. Like I said before, my mom always made sure I had a roof over my head, BUT times was definitely still not the best. It seemed like I always saw my mom struggling to make ends meet even with the help from my father and I know it wasn't easy feeding all three of us. Yes, three of us. Did I mention I had a brother and a sister? Somehow I always seems to forget to mention them.

We grew up in the same house since birth, same mama, different daddies, but it just never seemed like we had that sibling bond like other brothers and sisters. It was always some kinda of sibling rivalry going on. I watched other families and how they interacted with one another and I use to wish we was like that, but that never happened. After a while, I stopped wishing.

In a way, I always felt like the black sheep of the family and I was cool with that. Somebody gotta be it, right? So because I wasn't tight with my siblings it was easy for me to meet people and become really close to them. I learned how to make them the sisters and brothers that I never had. That's how I met my very first best friend in the whole wide world Tonya.

Growing up in the hood, families were always coming and going. I remember when Tonya and her family moved to the neighborhood. We were all outside playing in the street when this big ass moving truck came rolling down the block. It pulled up right across the street from my house. We all sat there watching and waiting to see what our new neighbors looked like. I saw a little brown girl hop out first. She looked like she was around my age, so I was excited.

It seemed like most of the kids on my street were either older or younger than me. I needed some new friends my age.

As her family started to unload the truck, she was just sitting on the porch looking like she could use a buddy, so I walked over to introduce myself.

"Hey, what's your name, I'm Kiesha."

"Tonya," she said, and that was pretty much the start of our friendship. Growing up things were so easy. You could just meet somebody, become friends and live happily ever after. Or so I thought...

Chapter 2

From the very first day we met, Tonya and I were stuck to each other's hips like glue. I mean we literally liked all of the same things—dancing, movies, racing and having lots of fun. We walked to school together every day, walked home from school together every day and as soon as we finished that homework, we were both back outside together every day. As I mentioned earlier, I really wasn't close to my own siblings, so I found myself getting drawn to other people—probably looking for some kind of connection. If and when my mother would ever be looking for me the first place she use to look was Tonya's house and vice versa. If I'm not mistaken she and I even kissed our first boys together.

I remember our first fight together too. My neighbors that lived upstairs cousins were staying there for the summer and oh what a summer that was. Every day they use to come outside and play in the backyard. They really never spoke, so we just assumed they didn't wanna play with us. While they played in the back, we played in the front because we needed to always see what was going on on the street. It wasn't a day that went by that Tonya and me wasn't sitting on my front porch hanging.

One day when we came out to play they was sitting in our spot in the front yard. When I tell you me and Tonya was on fire when we saw them, we felt real disrespected. Tonya was like

"Let's beat they asses up off the porch," Tonya remarked. That was the kinda person she was, rowdy-rowdy, bout it-bout it. Don't get me wrong, I was rowdy-rowdy too, but my mama was -bout it-bout it for real and was definitely gon beat my ass if I was outside fighting.

"Why don't we just ask em what they doing in the front? Let's just be chill."

The way Tonya was looking you could tell she wasn't on it, but she went along with it. We walked up to the front trying not to let it show we wasn't feeling them in our spot. We walked right up, sat down and Tonya was like, "So why y'all up here? Lol. I'm looking at her like, *Bitch that's what you came up with?* Bye girl. Before she could even finish what she was saying one of the cousins shot back, "Doing what the fuck we wanna do ugly!" I could not believe she just said that shit. See first of all, Tonya was far from ugly. Let's just start there. She had long pretty hair, brown skin and she was always showing them pretty white teeth off, smiling from ear to ear. I couldn't believe this bald-headed project-looking bitch had just tried to jump sharp with my bestie. I knew that it was only a matter of time before Tonya went the fuck off.

"Well first of all, you didn't have to get fly. I was just asking because this where we be chillin' and y'all know that." The cousin had the nerve to walk up to her and tell her we had to find another place to chill. Why did she tell her that. Tonya acted like she was bout to get up and leave, then turned around and smacked the dog shit outta her ass! Before I knew it the other cousin was jumping in and I was jumping right on that bitch neck! That was only like the second fight I had been in my whole life, but you couldn't tell. Long story short, that was our first fight together—definitely not our last and we was still sitting on the front porch after it was over and done so y'all can sorta assume who won. The rest of the summer they stayed they asses in the back.

That was the summer headed to 9th grade, which was also the year we met Dani who moved across the street from Tonya. This is when we started our first year in high school. Oh goodie.

Dani was a little different from us. Well not different, I'll say more advanced than us. Going into high school, Tonya and me still looked and acted like little girls. Boys just wasn't at the top of our list. We had a few boys checking for us and we had kissed a few and probably each let a few put they hands in our pants or some shit, but I think we was still immature in a lot of ways. Dani looked a little different. She had big ass titties and a big ass booty. The bitch looked like she been fucking all her life with hips and all. Meanwhile you could find us in the itty bitty titty committee, but we was still growing, at least that's what our parents use to tell us.

Going to high school was such a big deal. We thought it was time for us to start getting grown. We had seen Dani outside a few times but she never really came out to play. We got hip to her because all the boys in the neighborhood was talking about the new girl on the block. She was so strapped up everybody was trying to get at her.

One day we were all walking home from school and lil dirty ass Darnell pushed up on her and was trying to get her number. You can tell she was not interested by the way she kept looking at him. He kept on walking all close up on her then eventually decided to smack her on the ass. She turned around so quick and grabbed him by his shirt like he was her son and said, "If you ever put yo dirty ass paws on me again I'm a get my brother to knock your fucking teeth down your throat!" Me and Tonya was dead and started cracking the fuck up like, "Damnnnnnnn she checked the shit out that nigga." I had to give her props for that. That's the kinda shit we be on. Gotta constantly put these niggas in they place. When we saw that we ran and caught up to her and introduced ourselves. That's when two became three, that quick.

Snatch and Grab

Growing up in EC, your clique was your family. It was rules to this shit and we for sure had our own set. Don't mess with someone the other had talked to; if one fight we all fight; loyalty was everything and nothing could or should come between us, especially no niggas. That's how we met person number 4, Candy. Unlike all my other girls, we met Candy in a not-so-good kinda way.

I was dating this dude named Charlie and without me knowing he was dating Candy too. I found all this out one night we was all at a football game. Tonya, Dani and me was over by the bleachers smoking weed with the fellas which happened to be our favorite past time. After smoking a few blunts we had the munchies and decided we needed some snacks from the concession stand. As we were walking over there I saw Charlie talking to some thot. I knew I had to be high cause ain't no way in hell this nigga was crazy enough to be talking to a girl when he know I was somewhere around. I rubbed my eyes to make sure I wasn't tripping and when I saw them with a clear view I was heated.

For one, I was pissed that this nigga knew I was at the game and wanted to get on some disrespectful shit. For two, you over there about to buy this bitch some food? Nigga paleaseee! One thing you never do is buy another bitch some food. Oh it was on now.

I grabbed my purse and headed straight over to where they was talking. Of course you know my girls wasn't too far behind me.

"Uh, hello Charlie are you high or something, or this bitch gots to be your cousin?" This nigga was looking at me like he seen a ghost. "Hello? Charlie? Can you hear me? Earth to fucking Charlie!"

"Chill Stoney, you tripping."

"Tripping I ain't even started to trip yet nigga, who this hoe?"

"Excuse me, but my name is Candy," she chimed in, "and I don't see no hoes around here—well at least not this way." I was praying this girl ain't say shit—I really was hoping that she just stood to the side and said less, but nooooooo that was too much to ask.

"Listen, you have nothing to do with this so please just stay outta this, okay? Now back to you nigga, 'WHO THE FUCK IS THIS HOE!'" My finger was pointing all in his face. Man before I knew it this bitch, aka Candy, had punched me dead smack in my mouth and my shit starting leaking out the gate. After that, I couldn't even tell you what happened. She hit me, Tonya hit her, Charlie tried to break it up, Dani hit him and we all was fighting. The whole football game was now watching us instead of the game.

The Security guards and a few staff members rushed over and broke it up. My mouth was bleeding and I wanted to kill this hoe, and Charlie too. I'm thinking to myself, *This bitch gots to be crazy for stealing on me while my girls was right there. Did she think we was sweet or something?* The fuck. I was so mad security had broke up the fight. I wanted to kill her. After finally getting us all calmed down they asked her to explain what was going on since clearly she was by herself. Crazy thing is, when she started explaining she blamed lying ass Charlie for everything. She like: "Well it started when he started trying to talk to me knowing he had a girlfriend." She went on to say how she had told him to get away from her cause she didn't date cheaters. I was sorta sitting there feeling stupid cause I just might have overreacted, BUT I still had a busted lip so fuck that and fuck her.

They asked her how the fight had started and she was like, "I'm not sure, everything happened so quick, but I was feeling like they were going to do something to me so I sorta snapped and hit that one in the face," pointing to me. Then she went on to apologize to me and said she's not that kinda girl that just goes around swinging on people and she damn sure wasn't the type that dates people who are already in a relationship. It was weird cause even after this girl had just popped me dead smack in my mouth I sorta kinda felt like she wasn't the bad guy here. It was me—I was the bad guy.

I should have never came over there going off, calling her all sorts of hoes when in reality I should've just went straight over there and smacked Charlie in his fat face. I told her I was wrong and I was sorry. We all walked out together. Soon as security let us go I was like, "I need to get high now." Thing is, Dani had thrown the weed down the sewer when security was taking us back to the office. Fuck. The girl Candy looked back at us and was like "I got a bag," and that bag sealed the deal. We was a crew now. They said real niggas roll 4 deep right? It's crazy cause we all were completely different. Different backgrounds, different upbringings, yet at that time in life it felt like we were all the same. They say life comes at you fast but when you got a solid team you're ready for whatever. Or were we?

Chapter 3

Now that you've been introduced to the crew let's get to the money.

Living in East Cleveland, everybody pretty much had the same things. There weren't too many rich people in EC and if you was, why the hell were you still living there?

I noticed early on that most girls I grew up with didn't have fathers. For girls, that's a big deal. Dads are like a girl's first love. First guy to treat you good, first guy to make you happy and the first guy that sets examples for any other guy that enters your life.

My dad had a really good job and was a great provider, so he set thc bar high early for me. I never wanted for anything and I wasn't' missing any meals, but I didn't have all the designer bags and clothes that a lot of us wanted when we was younger. The school I went to had a dress code so from Monday thru Friday you looked the same as everybody else. It was the weekends when you saw who actually had them pieces on.

Me and my girls learned early to stand out instead of trying to fit in. We would go to the thrift stores and the local Goodwills to shop. They had all the designer shit, it just was the vintage version of it and we was cool with that because we didn't want to look like everybody else. We would go to the ones in the white neighborhoods where all the good shit use to be. We even made sure we went on the days that everything was half off so we could really get our shit for the low-low. So while everybody else was wearing name brands, we was creating a style of our own. It set us apart from everybody else. It also got us into fashion and learning more about designers. Even when we had to wear dress code we always, and I mean always, would put our own spin on our pieces.

High school in my eyes was very cloudy cause me and my girls went to school high every day. I smoked so much weed in high school I should've turned into a blunt. My crew was like the cool girls in school that everybody wanted to get high and hang out with. The dudes loved us and the girls hated us cause all the dudes liked us. Tonya and I were the two that smoked wayyyy too much weed, while Dani and Candy were the drinkers. At 16, we were leaving school getting drunk and high damn near every day of the week. It's crazy cause we would leave our houses dressed for a regular school day yet we never made it in the school. When I think back I be thinking, *What the fuck was wrong with us?* Y'all ever think, *What if?* What if I stayed in school, graduated and went straight to college? What kinda bitch would I be right now? Would I have become that lawyer I use to tell my mama and daddy I was gon be? Would I have married some smart guy I met in college and lived happily ever after? Or maybe my life was going exactly how it should be and I was right on schedule. Some days you just can't help but to wonder. I can say one thing though, me and my girls was NOT them fast-ass teenagers. We didn't get boy crazy till after high school. Yeah, we had niggas trying to fuck with us, but we was on some getting high tomboy shit.

At any given point you would catch us arguing, ready to fight some dudes. I think at one point we thought we was dudes. We wanted money way more than we wanted dick. I didn't even have sex 'til I was 16 and I think I only did it because of peer pressure. After that I didn't have sex again until I was 17, almost 18.

I remember I started talking to this older guy. He had to be every bit of 21 when we met. He was a friend of one of my friend's brother. Fly light-skinned cute nigga from the hood, and back then light-skin guys was everything. I thought he was the one.

When I met him we spent our first date just rolling around the hood smoking weed and talking. He was talking to me like he was my daddy and even though I had a daddy, I liked it. Telling me all kinds of things that a lady should and should not be doing. He was way older than me so I felt like I was just sucking up some game. I remember him lifting up my arms to see if I had hair under there. I felt so embarrassed when he saw I hadn't shaved. He said always keep yourself together from head to toe. A woman keeps things like her underarms shaved. Bet he never caught me like that again. He use to always stress the fact that a woman should always have her own money no matter what. Another thing he use to tell me was don't fuck with these niggas for free. I could hear him now: "If a nigga wanna lay down with you, he should be ready to make sure you good." Why would he tell me something like that? I was young and impressionable, and I was sucking up everything he was telling me. I don't think he ever knew how much his words would stick with me for life.

I respected him so much I knew he wouldn't tell me nothing wrong. I didn't know if he liked me for real or wanted to pimp me, but I took mental notes of everything he use to say. From that day on it was fuck niggas, get money, and I even started telling anybody that would listen that this pussy was not free. I sorta even started pushing it like it was for sale. To be exact, ain't no sorta about it. This pussy was definitely for sale.

Sometimes I think back to all the shit I did and ask myself would I change something, and every time I get the same answer. No. If I didn't go through all of the shit I went through I wouldn't, be the person I am today. Trials and tribulations builds character. So do selling pussy, or nah?

My life changed forever when I started boosting though. I can remember that day like it was yesterday. Tonya wanted to go get some new shoes from the mall and do some window shopping. We were about to leave school and do our same daily routine—cut and get high. This was our senior year and please don't even ask me how we made it to 12th grade when we never went to school. I think the school we went to had something called No Student Left Behind, meaning they would let you go to the next grade even if you didn't have the grades to pass. It was up to you to make sure you had all the credits you needed by senior year. You needed 16 credits to graduate. I think by 12th grade, I had 4. Don't judge me. Being that we never stayed at school, we was all down to go to the mall.

Dani's older brother had blessed her with a whip, so we was going and coming as we pleased. We hit up the weed man, stopped and got some shells and headed to the mall. Soon as we pull up to the mall Candy get to spraying all kinds of perfume and shit talking bout she don't wanna smell like weed. Why do people smoke hella weed then don't be wanting to smell like it??? It's impossible, but we always let her think she wasn't smelling like a Kush factory.

Ten minutes later, we all sitting in the shoe department looking high and stuck, watching Tonya be her regular indecisive-self looking at a million shoes. This was blowing my high big time. The only thing on my mind right then was getting something to snack on, but since we needed to pass time I told the homies *Let's go try on some prom dresses*. They was looking so high I think they would've been down for whatever long as we wasn't sitting in this shoe department.

Peep this though, this how you know we was high. We bout to go try on prom dresses when none of us was even graduating! I blame it on the weed. We probably tried on every dress in there just acting goofy, passing time.

I was headed out the dressing room to get some more dresses when Tonya called talking bout she couldn't find any shoes and she was hungry. I was greedy, so that was all I needed to hear. It was time to put these clothes back on quick, cause if I didn't eat something soon I was gon start being a bitch. I wasn't very nice when I was hungry—well at least that's what I heard.

When I was walking back to put my stuff on I noticed a black leather coat laying on the floor in an empty dressing room. I thought it must've been somebody's and maybe they forgot it. I hurried up and grabbed it, then took it back in my dressing room and shut the door. I'm going through the pockets until I saw it had a tag on it. That bitch was a $375 BCBG leather bomber—raw as fuck! Now I told y'all I never was the type that had expensive shit but I knew it when I saw it. It was my size too. I had never stole anything like that before. Lil shit from the neighborhood store maybe, but not a $400 coat.

I'm sitting in the dressing room just staring at it. I was nervous as shit and didn't really wanna tell the other girls because they would make me even more nervous. I almost jumped when my phone rang again. It was Tonya trying to see where I was at. Same time my phone was ringing Dani was banging on the dressing room door.

"C'mon Stoney," she whispered, urgently.

"Here I come girl, damn!"

I threw the coat in my purse, put my clothes back on and came out. Of course ,soon as I come out here go Dani whining about me taking forever and blah blah blah. I ain't hear shit she was saying.

I was scared to death, but I had to keep my composure. Never let them see you sweat, right? As we were walking out of the store I glanced at myself in the mirror. I really was trying to make sure nobody was following me, so I started fake fixing my hair. Did I say never let em see you sweat? Baby when I looked in the mirror my whole ass armpits was soaking wet! Oh, somebody was scared and it was just my luck we parked by the food court which was allllllll the way on the other side of the mall. Jesus!!! Somebody just shoot me now. Every security guard I saw I could've sworn he was looking at me and the worst part about it, I couldn't say shit to anybody. When we got in the car I'm like, "Dani hurry up and get us outta this area." Everybody looked at me like I was smoking something other than weed.

I pulled out the leather coat, smiling ear to ear like, "Look what I got." It was like we was at a museum or something how we all was looking at the coat.

"Is that a BCBG coat bitch?" Dani's mouth was wide open after she said that.

"Yep, sure is and its $375."

"How in the fuck did you get that? Naw, fuck that, when did you get it? You never even went to that section." Tonya was so lost. I started explaining.

"Soooooo, when we was in the dressing room trying on dresses I saw it laying on the floor in one of them empty dressing rooms. I grabbed it and took it back to my room. It didn't have no beepers, no ink thingies—nothing. I just folded that bitch up and put it in my purse. Nobody was even helping us and nobody was out there when I came out the dressing room." We still was all just looking at the coat in awe.

"What you gon do with it, keep it? Of course Dani wanted to know that part cause she probably wanted to wear it. "Hell naw, I'm selling this bad baby, fuck that. If its $375, I'm sure one of these boujie hairstylist wouldn't have no problem giving me $200 for it, what y'all think?" Candy like, "I know somebody that'll buy it right now." She picked up her phone and started making some calls. I was still shook a little from it all and needed to get high.

"Somebody blaze up please."

Candy was still trying to find me a sale when we pulled up to meet the weed man. Yeah we needed more already I told you don't judge us. Weed always kept me cool, calm and collective. I'm in the backseat still tripping that I had just stole this jacket. I felt scared, but for real I felt like a rebel.

We all put our coins together so once we pulled up on him we could just get our sack and pull out. Soon as he came up to the car, first thing he said was, "Who selling that coat?" I'm like, "Me. Why you want it?"

"My girl like all that fancy designer stuff. Let me call her and see what size she wear." He hit his girl up and won't he don't it, she wore a medium, the same size as the jacket. "How much you want?"

"Two hundred."

He picked up the coat and looked at it again. "Lemme give you $175 and a nice ass bag of this grandpa haze." I think the words *A'ight* came out my mouth so fast I almost lost the sale. I gave him the coat, he gave me the money and the sack of weed and we pulled off. I was 17 at the time and I had never in my life made $200 that fast. It felt good. The looks in me and my girl's eyes was the look of greed and excitement all in one. Without saying nothing, we all knew it was on and popping.

We went back to Tonya's house and that was the best session of our lives, cause all we did was make plans and talk about getting to this money. We really sat there making plans on how we was bout to start stealing from these malls and get us some money. That was the first day of many more missions—money-getting-missions, that is.

Chapter 4

Our 12th grade year was spent getting at that knot. I told y'all none of our parents had money for real. Our families were like most inner city kids families in the neighborhood—we had a roof over our heads, food on our tables and we'd better be thankful for that. Asking for extra shit was pushing it. When we started getting this boosting money we ain't know what to do. After I sold that first BCBG coat and touched that fast cash, we were hooked. We decided we was gone stick to stealing high end things so we knew we was always gon get a nice lil penny. The designer shit was always priced high as fuck so whatever we sold it for was gone be nice regardless.

We was leaving out them stores everyday with all kinds of pieces; BCBG, Banana Republic, Roberto Cavalli, all that. Hell, one time we got our hands on some Versace stuff. You couldn't tell us nothing. We had made it to the major leagues of stealing.

You want to hear the craziest shit? We hardly ever kept any of it. We wanted that money baby. We had this rule though, that we would never all go in together—didn't wanna look hot and suspicious four deep. So two would go in while the other two stayed out. Once they came out the other two went in like clockwork. We use to plan this shit out perfectly everyday like we was bout to go rob a bank. We started building up a crazy clientele too. Word gets around quick when you got some nice pieces going for nice prices.

Bitches that never liked me was even hitting me up. I felt like Mystikal: "You looking for me, here I go!"

Business was booming and we was loving every minute of it. We started making a name for ourselves in the streets. People knew if they needed some good shit, hit us up. We started off putting the stuff in our purses but as we got better and better and had bigger orders to fill we started using shopping bags and learned how to stuff them properly. We would leave these stores with big bags loaded with stuff. We was getting women's and men's clothes and if you knew exactly what you wanted we was getting baby clothes too. The money started coming real fast to the point we couldn't keep nothing at all. Soon as we was getting it they was buying it. Everything too. I could easily make $500-$700 a day. Honestly some of us was making more than our parents did doing this shit and they never even knew. I remember one day my mom call herself washing all my clothes. No one asked her to do it, but when you still living at home what can you expect? I had a few hundred dollars in the back pocket of a pair of jeans I had taken off the night before. When she went to turn my jeans inside out she discovered the bread and called my ass right up, asking me where I got it from. She said she hoped I wasn't doing anything illegal to get it. Of course I lied and told her one of my male friends gave it to me to get a new cellphone cause the one I had was broke, now put my money back where you got it from please. I knew right then it was time for me to get up outta her shit. School had just let out for summer too. We was all 18, and independence was sounding real nice. I was ready to get my own everything. My own crib, whip, man, and anything else I could buy. Money was plentiful and I felt like nothing could stop this train.

When you come from nothing then start getting your own money, I don't think it's a better feeling than that. Being able to buy things we never could before was a blessing if you asked me. Yeah, it was illegal, but at least we weren't stealing from people. We were stealing from stores who had all that shit insured.

We went from eating Ramen Noodles to steaks and shrimp every day of the week. We was in so deep we had started stealing food from the grocery stores too. We had learned a new way to get money, but it was a new way to survive, for real.

Everyday I came home from hustling, I was putting a few dollars to the side because I needed everything once I moved. New bedroom, couches, dishes, you know, the things a home need.

My mom started tripping hard about me coming in and outta her house all times of the night. I was hustling so hard I was barely there, only coming there to sleep and that's about it. I think she was tripping so hard cause she knew something was going on with me. She just couldn't figure out what.

She had no idea I had already gave someone a first months rent and deposit. I was just waiting for the right time to tell her.

After one long ass day of hustling I goes home and guess who up on bullshit? Mom dukes.

"Since you and your little friends are making all this money, I'm going to need you to start paying rent around here. You're not going to be laying around here for free. You hear me?"

"I'll be out of here by the first, okay Ma?" I told her looking her dead in her eyes. She was quiet as a mouse. I started to say, *Do you hear me?* but I wasn't that disrespectful kid. It just felt like that would've been a good time to say that.

She probably couldn't believe I was taking my talents up outta her shit. I been tired of living by her rules anyway. Tired of sneaking around, trying to hide all that stolen shit without her seeing it. If I thought I was so grown it was time for me to go be grown and pay some grown-ass bills. I sure was making enough to be paying somebody's rent. Not to mention, along with boosting I was working niggas too. I couldn't be doing all that up out of mommy do shit.

I still don't think my mother even believed me until moving day. She thought I was just talking. By the time the 1st came, I done stole damn near everything for my house except the furniture itself.

See at first we started stealing clothes, but once we learned that the hands is quicker than the eyes chile we was taking anything that wasn't nailed down. Groceries, appliances, house goods, jewelry, all that. You might think I'm lying, but one time my girl stole a $2,500 poodle from the pet store. Shit was just wild at that point. We was young and living our lives like we couldn't be touched.

We wasn't like kleptomaniacs though. Somebody could leave their purse around me and I wouldn't even think about going in it. We stole to make money and that's it. Wasn't no addiction and we didn't get high off the adrenaline. We got high off the weed y'all could keep that adrenaline. No ma'am. I was so excited and so ready to be on my own. I mean, I was 18 and at that age I was bout to be able to do what I wanted, and with who I wanted without nobody checking for me. I was soooooooo ready to move into my own place. At least I thought I was.

When moving day came around, I had everything together. The last thing I wanted was to show my mother I wasn't prepared. I had my U-Haul, my movers and already packed everything. There really wasn't much there but a bunch of things I had growing up. The bedroom set I had was the same set I had since I was 14. That mutha fucka was not going anywhere with me. All I was taking was clothes and shoes.

My mother threatened to kick me out on many occasions and said over and over again she wanted me out, BUT the day I was actually getting out she was looking like she didn't really want me to go. Probably realized a lot of her extra money was bout to walk out the door. I was only moving 15 minutes away, but this was bout to be my very first apartment. For my mom, I was the last one in the house, so this move was bout to be different for everybody.

I spent that whole day moving. I wanted everything to be perfect. At about 11 o'clock that night we was finally done. I paid the movers, aka the crackheads and I locked up. I turned around and just stared at my cute little apartment. I had my own shit! My own apartment that didn't nobody help me get. Damn, I felt independent as fuck!

I sat on my couch, picked up the remote and turned the TV on. This was definitely a whole vibe. Before I could even get deep into my chill, I heard somebody knocking at the door. Of course, y'all know who that was. My mutha fucking girlsssss. I opened the door so quick, ready to welcome the crew into my new bachorlette pad. Tonya was the first one in of course. "I got champagne and Kush. It's a celebration bitches.

"Damnnnnnn Stoney this spot dope, Yup it's official I gotta start looking for me one, you just motivated me bitch."

Sitting there sipping Ciroc, bubbly and smoking on that good bag in my new spot with the homies was feeling like everything at the moment. I felt like Scarface, like the world was mines. Well maybe not Scarface. More like Regine from Living Single. To me this was what hard work looked like. I had hustled for about 2-3 months and wasn't spending shit. Took my time trying to find a nice apartment that wasn't in the hood, but wasn't too far from everything. I was proud of myself. Proud that I had put my mind to something and actually followed through with it. Shit felt pretty damn good too. That night we stayed up all night getting lit and enjoying my new home. Life wasn't bad at all. Matter fact, it was pretty damn good.

Chapter 5

Let me be the first to tell you that with money comes a lot of things: greed, jealousy, betrayal, all that. Money will turn your own mama on yo ass for the right price. One thing I can say about me and my crew—we was all solid. We wasn't about to let any amount of money break up our bond. Or so I thought.

We was fresh out of high school and all doin' pretty well for ourselves. I mean, at least in our eyes we was. I enjoyed being in a place where if I wanted something I knew I could just hustle and go get it. I loved getting money, but that shit didn't make me. I would help any and everybody if I could. I'm the type of person that would give you my last without you even knowing its my last cause I knew it wasn't shit to get it right back.

I sometimes felt like that was a gift and a curse because you can't help everybody cause when you down and need somebody to help you them same people gon be sounding like crickets. I always told myself to never get too wrapped up in the hustle that you stopped caring about everything else around you. I learned not to cherish materialistic things cause they could all be replaced.

Speaking of that, I remember this one time when me and Dani fought in my house. We had all been out hustling all day and decided we was gon meet up and cook at my spot. We all loved seafood, so we was gon make some of them seafood boil bags. We just wanted to chill, smoke and throw down.

After we all busted a few sales we met back up at my house. People have no idea how tiresome it is running in and out of them malls all damn day. Driving all across the fucking world trying to swindle these people out they shit—playing all kinds of games to get this money. Then you gotta deal with all the people you sell the shit too. They wanna get all kinda deals, not respecting the fact that you just risk your whole life to get all this stuff out of the stores. This life was so much more than people really saw and it wasn't for everybody. We went damn near everyday of the week, plus the weekends. This was our jobs and we was putting in way more hours than 40 a week. This game is for true hustlers. Your money depends on you.

It was plenty days I done went to 6-7 malls in one day. We'd start at 9am when they opened and literally would be leaving out them stores at 9pm when they close. Some days I would get up and dread getting on them roads. I don't even wanna talk about the missions within itself. While you out on the road you need gas, weed, food etc. So yeah, by the time we was finished hustling all day we just wanted to relax and see how much money we made. We was at my house, chilling making seafood. About a week prior to that I had went and copped a new, big ass TV. I can't even remember what size it was. I was just at Walmart one day and seen it was on sale and copped it. It looked good sitting in my front room too.

We all was just sitting around kicking it, smoking, waiting for the food to get ready. Dani who was clearly wasted started telling us some story about some nigga she seen at the mall and blah blah blah. We sitting there cracking the fuck up cause she telling the story, but she being so extra cause she geeked. She ended up doing some kinda spin thing and fell into my brand new tv and pushed it off the stand and broke my shit. Y'all know I was super upset. For one, I've never been a heavy drinker and I hateeeee when people can't handle they liquor. I jumped up like, *What the fuck!* I knew she didn't mean to do it, but I was still mad as shit.

"Dani what the fuck man damnnnn!"

At this point I was yelling cause I was extremely salty. My brand new TV just laying on the floor shattered. I know steam had to be coming out of my ears cause I was on fire. "Oh yo drunk ass gon have to buy me another TV, period."

Dani gets up off the couch still tipsy apparently, and out of nowhere gets to talking crazyyy.

"Girl I'll buy you another TV, that ain't shit. I might have one for you laying around at the house. I keep big TV's baby."

I'm looking at this girl like you can't be serious. You broke my TV now you in my house talking crazy as fuck. Wowwwwwwwww! She was clearly drunk, but it sounded like she was feeling some kinda way about some other shit too. I'm looking at her like, *Girl you is tripping and you need to calm the fuck down.* She kept just going off and yelling and talking about a bunch of silly shit.

"You always tripping thinking you better than somebody else," she said. "We all make mistakes. Chill the fuck out before I MAKE you chill out."

Now listen, I know I said we was all like sisters and whatnot, but this bitch was beginning to press her luck. *Bitch you just broke my brand new TV, you in my house talking wayyyyy too loud and now you talking bout fighting?* I walked straight up to her and told that hoe if she didn't lower her mutha fucking voice we was gone have a big problem. Before I even finished, she smacked the fuck outta me right in my face! When I said I tried to kill that hoe that night you gotta believe me. I grabbed her by her hair so quick and started pounding on that head. I don't know if I beat her ass cause she broke my TV, or the fact that she was up in my shit talking to me like she was nuts. Tonya and Candy tried breaking it up, but we was fighting-fighting, She had me by my hair, but I was drilling her so fucking hard in her face I thought I was gon kill her. I think the only reason we broke that shit up was because I heard somebody banging at my door. Sounded like them police kinda knocks.

We both let go of each other and I ran and got the door. It was the lady from downstairs trying to see what was going on up there. I told her I was cool and we was good, but my hair was all over the place and I was looking like I was fighting. Why was we just fighting like that? If we supposed to be sisters, why we fighting each other like some random bitches on the streets? Weed and drink was spilled all over the floor, and we broke two of the candles on the table.

I went to my bedroom and slammed the door. I couldn't even be in the same room with her right now cause for real I wanted to go beat that ass again. How dare you come up in my shit talking crazy and then raise your hand to smack me? Bet that bitch think twice before she does that again. Now my neighbors probably think I'm some ghetto ass girl who be having too much going on in her apartment. If I get a call from my landlord, I know something. That was not the kind of attention I wanted living in my new spot.

Tonya knocked on my door and came in. She knew I was heated cause she knew me the longest. She knew all my secrets, all my dreams, what I liked, what I didn't like, and she damn sure knew when I was mad af. She just came in and was staring at me. I ain't even wanna look up at her cause I was just too mad at that point. When I looked up she just busted out laughing. I tried so hard not to laugh, but this bitch thought everything was funny. "Bitchhhhhhh, what the fuck is you hoes into?" she said, smiling. I couldn't help but to crack a smile cause we definitely was just in my house fighting like some damn dogs.

I looked at Tonya and asked her flat out, "Was I wrong?" cause I know sometimes I've been known to overreact. But Dani hadn't even said sorry or nothing. Just went straight in. Not to mention it sounded like she had a lot of animosity she wanted to get off her chest. I always hated when you get into it with someone and they start telling you how they really feel. That shit be making me wanna beat yo ass even more.

I was feeling a type of way. Me and Dani ain't never messed with the same dudes, never stepped on each others toes over no money, nothing, so it was hard for me to figure out where this hoe was coming from.

"Yeah she was dead ass wrong, but both of y'all just needed to calm down. It went left quick. Y'all need to squash that shit and talk it out immediately."

One thing about me is I wasn't good at being fake. If I was feeling some kinda way about anything I always had to address it cause suppressing it is not an option. I didn't have a problem talking it out with Dani, but we was definitely gon get to the bottom of this. Tonya and I walked back into the front room where Dani and Candy was sitting. Candy was rolling up some weed while Dani was just sitting there looking simple. I swear that liquor be a mutha fucka. I'm almost positive that if she hadn't been drinking she would've never popped off like that.

Tonya stood up: "Okay, clearly we may have had a little too much to drink. Dani you had wayyyyyyy too much to drink, but we is sisters and sisters do NOT fight each other. We get money together, play niggas together, hit these licks together. We got Stoney's neighbors all in the business. They could've called the police then we would've had more problems then we wanted." Tonya was trying to reason and diffuse the situation. She continued, "Y'all gotta squash this shit ASAP.

"I'm not about to sit up here and go back and forth about this shit," I said. "Dani broke my mu fucking TV and instead of just saying sorry, she went completely left talking bout her TV at home bigger and I stay on bullshit and all kind of other shit. I'm trying to figure out what the real problem is cause I can get another TV with no problem. But if it's some smoke in the air we need to clear that shit up."

Dani was still looking drunk but she was also looking like she was about to cry.

"I'm sorry," was the first thing that came out her mouth before she just busted out in tears. "I'm sorry, I don't know what's been going on with me lately. I just been feeling lost as fuck, like my life isn't going anywhere. I been frustrated as hell and that's why I been drinking so much. Stoney, I am sorry man. I wasn't never supposed to take it where I just did. I don't have no issues with you. I love you so much. I'll get you another TV sis, please except my apology." By this point I was damn near in tears too. You don't never know what somebody is going through, especially if you ain't asked em how they doing? I went over and just hugged her. I had been so caught up in my own life that I probably wasn't even thinking about anybody else's. I think black folks tend to do that a lot—get so wrapped up in doing them that they forget to see if errbody else cool. Imma just keep it 100 though. Yes I forgave Dani for breaking my TV and for being on bullshit, but I was definitely giving her the side eye about all that shit she was saying. People always said a drunk speaks the truth and I believed that. She had some kinda hidden beef with me and I wasn't going to act like she didn't. Yeah, I accepted her apology, BUT I was gone keep my eyes open real wide when it came to her. I no longer trusted my sis.

Chapter 6

When I think back to my childhood friendships, I see a bunch of lost lil girls that was so tough on the outside, but all broken in our ways on the inside. We was hard as fuck on each other when we needed to be pouring into each other.

Hands down, the biggest issues with friendships and relationships is communication. I hate when somebody come tell me some shit that one of my so called friends said, but I'm the last one to know. That be that fake bs. I can admit I'm a little more aggressive than the average woman. I just don't like taking people's shit and most of the time I can see right through it.

Ever since me and Dani had fought it was a little awkwardness in the crew. I could tell Candy was in her feelings now too. Tonya even noticed it and said something to Candy about it. All she could say was, "I think Stoney took that too far." Wow, I took it too far when I was clearly attacked? All of it just showed me that everybody wasn't as real as they claimed to be. I wasn't gon let that stop me from doing me.

I didn't have a car yet, so I had started paying other people to take me to the mall unless me and Tonya went and hit a lick. I started looking for people who needed some extra money. The lifestyle I was living showed me that money made people move a little faster.

One of my faithful customers that always use to cop from me had recently told me she got laid off from her job so she wouldn't be having no money any time soon. She was the perfect person for the job. I hit her up and asked her if she wanted to make $100 by taking me to the mall. You would've thought I called her and told her she won the Publisher's Clearinghouse Sweepstakes or something. She was so excited she told me she would head my way immediately. It was 9 at night and wasn't no damn mall even open, crazy ass.

She got to telling me how broke she was and needed money to feed her kids and how I called her at the right time. She was cool, but she was little bit crazy. I swear nowadays everybody be saying they crazy, so when they do bullshit they can blame it on that. I don't be buying that shit. Get yo crazy ass knocked out.

I wasn't bout to kiss Dani ass for a ride to the mall. Fuck her and fuck her ride too. No matter what was going on in my life I've always been the kind of girl that was always looking for solutions. Maybe it was the Capricorn in me or maybe just the hustler in me, but I strongly believed where there's a will there's a way.

It was gon be different going to the mall with someone different for the first time, but I needed to get this money so I could get me a car. I told her come swoop me up around 10 in the morning and I hung up. She was still talking when I hung up.

The next morning ole girl picked me up and we headed out. I could tell out the gate this was about to be an aggravating mission cause the bitch couldn't drive. She kept swerving and speeding and when you on a mall mission ain't none of that allowed. The last thing you want to do is bring any kind of unwanted attention to you. I let her know quick, baby this ain't that. For 100 dollars you need to make sure I get to where we going safely and slow this bitch down. She was looking at me a lil crazy like who this bitch think she talking to and I was looking right back at her like youuuu. When we got to the mall I had a pep talk with her.

"You don't have to do anything. Just watch me. If you see something you want just tell me. Do not steal shit, don't wonder off, and do NOT be on your phone. This is some serious shit and I don't got time to be playing." It was funny cause she was looking at me like I was crazy—probably never knowing the job was so planned out and serious. Yes bitch it was, and I wasn't trying to catch a case due to your stupidity.

Soon as we stepped one foot in the mall she said she had to go to the bathroom. She was bout to drive me crazy I could see. I showed her where it was and I went to check out some of the stores to see if I knew any of the workers, or should I say, see if any of them knew me. Not sure what y'all thought be happening in them stores, but it's not easy at all. People be like, *When you gone get my stuff?* Girrrlll, when they let me get it. You had to be patient with this mall shit. Go in at the right time. You had to watch the workers, the customers and people walking through the mall. That's why it was good to go with somebody else. Four eyes was always better than two. And speaking of four eyes, where the hell was my other set?

I look up she in Auntie Annie's line. Why me. I usually made a mental list of the things I wanted to get so I could go in with a plan. On that day I just wanted to get a bunch of jeans, some baby clothes for my homie and about a million candles. Candles was my biggest lick. Everybody loved candles and them bitches was not cheap. If I didn't get nothing else I made sure I got some of them.

We slid in the first store where I was gone grab my one old-school lady a bunch of work clothes. The store was a little crowded so it looked like I came at the perfect time. Hold up, where was my other set of eyes?

I turn around looking for this lady and you will not believe what she was doing. Take a guess please? This bitch was putting a shirt in her purse and the dumb bitch didn't even see that it had a beeper still on it. Clearly this ain't yo lane, you don't know what you doing, not to mention I told yo simple ass before we came to keep your hands to yourself. If you stealing, you can't possibly be watching me. Stick to the script.

Not gone even lie, my girls and I turned a lot of girls out to boosting. They would see the money and be like, *I can do that*, not knowing how much came with this shit. I mean, hell, the shit held jail time need I say more?

I was salty as fuck when I saw her put that shirt in her purse. She wasn't even checking her surroundings or nothing, just reckless. I went over there and she jumped when she saw me pull up right behind her. "How you over here watching my back when I should be the one watching your back. You boost now too huh?"

She started rambling about how she just needed a shirt and it looked like it was sweet. I asked her was she planning on taking that censor off. From her facial expressions you can tell she didn't even know it had a censor. Next thing you know one of the workers came over talking about could she help us and it just so happened to be one of the workers who hated me. We would go in and out of these stores so much they had to know something. They was just waiting to catch us in the act.

"No ma'am, we good just looking for something to wear to my moms anniversary party." I always made up some of the most extravagant stories. I told my girl get rid of that shirt and let's go.

I never was the one to trip on too many things, BUT when it came to my money I was a completely different person. This dummy had just fucked up that whole lick and I was NOT a happy camper. She came out the store looking goofy like she ain't know what had just happened. I got straight to the point

"Listen I'm paying you a 100 bucks to watch my fucking back, not steal your own shit. If you wanna go stealing go by yourself, but if you think for one second I'm going to give you 100 dollars and you not even doing your job you out your rabbit-ass mind." She got that shit together real quick, thinking about that $100 walking right outta her life. I was so irritated I just bust a few moves and was ready to go. I wasn't bout to let nobody else get me hot and security get called or something. I had never been to jail, never been caught and didn't wanna start now.

The reason I hadn't been to jail was because I wasn't thirsty. If I went somewhere and it didn't look like I could get anything I would just leave, unlike my girls. They felt like, *You gon give me this shit one way or another.* They were more of the aggressive boosters. That ain't how I got down though. I'd take whatever I could get and call it day before I got greedy and caught a case.

On our way driving home I had my mind made up that I was gon hustle my ass off for the next two weeks so I could cop me a whip. I couldn't be going on missions like this with people like this. Shit always goes wrong when you don't stick to the script, not to mention I think this girl was slow. She whistled every song that came on the radio the whole ride home. Yep, it was official, this was her first and last hunnit she would ever get from me. I sold my shit, gave her the money I promised, and got dropped off at home. When I was getting out she had the audacity to say, "Same time tomorrow right?" I shut the door and acted like I ain't even hear her. *Take care, sticky fingers,* is what I was thinking. Walked in the house and couldn't wait to kick off my shoes and light up my blunt. Soon as I got to tasting my weed my phone starting ringing. I wasn't about to get up, but something told me I should answer it. It was Tonya and she was talking so fast I could barely even understand her.

"Slow the fuck down, what happened?" She took a deep breath and told me.

"Candy got caught stealing. She's in jail."

Chapter 7

Seems like even though we had something going on at that time, none of it mattered cause we all got together immediately. Dani and Tonya was at my house before I could even hang up. They busted in my shit like the police was after them too.

"What the fuck happened?" I said, after they busted in the door. I'm looking at Tonya but Dani started talking first.

"Girrrllll, we was at the mall and this was the last spot we was gone hit. We had just tore they ass up but Candy wanted to go back in to get this order she said for her dude." I started shaking my head cause it always be some fuck shit like that, I swear. She continued: "We went back in and when we was leaving out we saw the sales associate that worked there hop on the phone looking real sneaky. I told Candy let's go but she thought I was just being noided. I'm walking fast and she on her phone talking about she wanted some Auntie Annie's. I knew she was lying or playing thee fuck outta crazy. I'm like I'm going to the car then."

"If you ask me, I think she was trying to get some more shit for her dude daughter. I went and sat in the car and just waited for her to come out," Dani added. While I'm sitting there, I see the police pull up and hop out and damn near run in the mall. I'm calling Candy phone like crazy, but of course, as usual her phone was dead. I tell this hoe every time to keep her phone charged, but clearly she don't listen. I got so scared I pulled to another parking spot just in case they was looking for me. Shit, like 7 minutes later, I saw them walking out the mall with Candy in handcuffs. I got thee fuck outta there as fast as I could before they started looking for me if they wasn't already."

OMG. None of us had ever caught a case before. It's been a few times we thought someone was on to us or a few times security may have looked like they was bout to be on trash but each time we dipped out and nothing came of it.

Most of the times we thought we probably was just paranoid but it's better to be safe than sorry.

"I know y'all got some weed, a bitch is stressed," I said, leaning back on my couch. What jail she in? We got to get her out." Dani was sitting there looking so stuck, she could barely get her thoughts together.

"We was at Beachwood Mall girl."

I grabbed the Swisher and broke it down. Them folks did NOT play out there. I barely even went to that spot to hit my licks. Too many police was always there on trash. I picked up the phone and called Beachwood jail so I could see what we needed to do to get her out. As I sat there rolling that blunt trying to get all the information I needed from the police, I was just thinking about everything. Would I be going crazy if I was Candy? What's gon happen next? That's why I smoke weed so much, cause it kept me sane in situations like this. I blazed up the blunt and hung up the phone. "Police said she won't have a bond 'til after she go to court in the morning and it's probably gon be about $1,500 for her to get out." Man, I could not believe it was bout to cost that much to get her out of jail. I think between all of us we had about $800 and a bunch of shit we could sell to probably get the rest. Candy probably had a couple dollars on her so we just had to wait 'til she got a chance to call to let us know what was up. My head was spinning. This shit had me shook. All I kept thinking about was, *What if it was me?*

I might be tough and strong minded, but I couldn't see myself in jail with a bunch of studs trying to take me down. Noooooooooo. This probably was the quietest sessions we ever had. We just sat there smoking waiting for Candy to call. The last couple weeks for the crew been real sketchy. Everybody been just doing they own thang, but now we was just all trying to figure out what was next.

Dani's phone starting ringing and we already knew that had to be Candy. Soon as she picked up you could here Candy crying. She put her on speaker.

"Candy c'mon stop crying, you know soon as they give you a bond we coming to get you, chill." Candy was already a crybaby, so I'm sure she was going crazy in that place.

"Aye man we can't go back to Beachwood y'all, they hip to us. They know our names and everything," Candy said over the phone. *Who names?* I thought. I know Candy might have been a little discombobulated, but hoe they don't know our names. We wasn't even with you sis. She better gone with all that." She continued: "Listen I'm telling y'all, they said the sales associate from the store told the police that I come in there all the time and I'm always with some other girls. Said two weeks ago I was in there with two girls and after we left they found some censors in the back of a pair of jeans. They've been waiting on one of us of to come back ever since. So today I really didn't even do no hot shit. They was on our ass from last week.

"See now this that shit I don't like. You telling me that I wasn't even at the scene of the crime and my name is involved. I know you lying. "So I go to court at 9am in the morning. Dani do not bring your ass up here. They kept asking me where you was and what your name was. I told them you was a crackhead and I paid you to take me to the mall." Tonya looked at the phone crazy

"Bitch you couldn't think of shit else to say. You done told the police she was a fiend? Wowwwww.

"I could've told em her name, so relax." Just call up here in the morning and get me thee fuck outta here, I gotta go." She hung up so quick we still had questions to ask, like number one, *What did you have on this bond?* Once again ,we was all sitting there looking stupid.

"Look y'all, we got to start being real careful and start going to some malls far out. Fuck all that inner city shit. If Candy telling the truth it could've been any of us that went down today. I'm not trying to go to jail no time soon." Both of their heads were shaking in agreeance. "Anybody got Candy dude number? He gone have to come up off some ends, especially since this bitch was being greedy going to get his lil kids some clothes." I wish the fuck I would.

We sat there smoking and talking for a while, but they both ended up just passing out on the couch. I gave em a few throw blankets and got in the bed. That night, I could not sleep a bit. I was wondering was the girls feeling like me—stomach all knotted up. I'm lying in bed pooting and shit cause I was scared. On some real shit, I was thinking maybe I needed to find a new hustle—another way to get some money. I did not want to end up in jail. You would think I was thinking something like, "Stoney it's time for you to get a job and start planning for your future," or "Stoney, maybe you should go back to school. You always wanted to be a writer, go take that journalism course you been looking up." Yeah, none of them ideas came to mind. I guess when you get in them streets your mind forgets all the good stuff you wanted to do and could do. It's like you only think of other ways to hustle. In my mind, I was feeling like I wanted out, but my heart was so street it was telling me just find a new hustle. I just said a prayer and fell asleep.

Chapter 8

That next morning Candy was on our phones blowing them babies up. The police dude was right—her bond was definitely $1,200 dollars. We had got $700 from her dude so we all went in on the rest. Tonya and I decided to go pay it while Dani stayed her ass in the crib. Beachwood be on that bullshit—fuck around and arrest her ass in the parking lot.

We paid her bond and waited outside forever talking bout they had to do a 50-state check on her. We sat in that parking lot looking like we was on America's Most Wanted, kept looking around every time we saw somebody pull up. Just being in the police station parking lot was giving me anxiety.

Finally, we saw Candy come out. When she saw us she started running. Her weave was looking slightly mangled and she looked like she stank but we was happy as hell to see her. She hopped in and was like, "Where the fuck the weed at. Get me the fuck out of here." We slid out that parking lot like thieves in the night. I couldn't even wait, I was thirsty to hear the story.

Only thing we knew was what Dani told us and she was on the outside looking in. We wanted to know what happened in the mall and how she got caught. She kept screaming blaze up blaze up

"Look, we not blazing shit up in Beachwood. To be exact we didn't even bring the weed with us. Simmer yo fresh-outta-jail-ass down and tell us what happened. We'll smoke back at the house. Dani got you one rolled up waiting." Tonya turned down the music so we could hear everything.

"Girl me and Dani was out kicking it the night before so neither of us even wanted to go to the mall, but we was broke as fuck. I wanted to go somewhere out the way, but Dani didn't feel like driving far and I didn't either. On God, I was laying in the bed and something was telling me to just take the day off. Dani hit me up talking bout she broke and needed some money to pay her phone bill. I had a soft $200 but I was just pressed to make some more. I should've stayed in the bed damn. We went to a few malls and none of em was really hitting, but we got a lil something from every one. I have no idea why Dani wanted to go to Beachwood. I even asked her what made her pull up in that bitch. She like, 'It's late its probably gone be shweet, blah blah blah. Long story short, we go up in there, hit a few spots then we hit Baby Gap. We get to the car and I wanted to go back in onlyyyyy because didn't nobody see me in Gap. So we went back in, I hit the lick and on our way out Dani said something like some white woman got on her phone. She didn't say some white woman got on her phone looking like she was bout to call the police. We leave out, I keep looking back. I don't see no white woman, security, nobody, so I went and got me some Auntie Anne's. I know, it's all my fault. I'm greedy and fat and that's why I got caught. I'm standing in the Auntie Anne line drinking my lemonade waiting for my pretzel and Beachwood police and the white woman walk right up on me. It was curtains after that. The cop told me to follow him to the back. I ain't even get to get my fucking pretzel, man. Bet money I drunk that whole lemonade before we even made it to the back though. I knew that was bout to be my last drink for the night. After that they took me to the back and asked me about some clothes and looked in my bags and told me I was going to jail."

I'm sitting here listening to the story like, Okkkayyy, now what about the part you said somebody said something about us famlee? I spoke up: "Didn't you say somebody remembered us or knew us or something chile? You done had me up all night worried to death."

"Uh, I was bout to say that part. The lady from Gap said we came in there a few weeks ago and hit em up and they knew we did cause when we left they found some jeans full of sensors in it."

"It wasn't us," I said, "but it sure sounded like us. We always put the sensors we pop off in the pockets of some jeans or jacket.

After listening to Candy's story it sounded like she was lightweight feeling a type a way about Dani. I sensed some tension in the air.

"Well we bout to go back to my house, hopefully Dani done whipped some shit up to eat while we was gone.

"Oh Dani there? Good, cause for real she the reason I got caught." I knew it. I knew Candy was on something. It's crazy cause people be quick to put the blame on somebody else knowing damn well they was wrong.

"Okay, if Dani wanted to go to Beachwood that didn't mean you had to double back in the Gap on some thirsty shit, but now you want to blame Dani. This was bout to be good. I wasn't even going to get in the middle of this shit cause my mind was already racing. I damn sure wasn't bout to let them work my nerves.

We walked in my house smelling the sweet smell of some swine. I knew Dani hungry ass had made something. She loved to be greedy like me. Soon as Candy walked in she was on bullshit coming through the door. "If we would have never went to Beachwood I would NOT have went to jail last night. I'm aggravated as fuck. Dani turned around and immediately got right back with her. "Are you kidding me right now Candy? Are we really about to do this? We made it out with all that shit and you was pressed as fuck to go back and get that nigga some shit!

"Aye, aye, aye, I'm not even bout to get in the middle of this, but we not about to get loud in my crib. Last time shit ain't end right a'ight." Candy sat her ass down and just laid back on the couch. "Maybe I'm just tripping—I'm just salty as fuck right now. I got to go to court for this shit. They said Beachwood gives every first offender jail time for stealing, no questions asked. How many days he gives you is up to him."

"Damn, first offenders get mandatory jail time? I'm never stealing from Beachwood again," I remarked.

Yes girl, it's on my paperwork. These bastards don't play. They make an example out of yo ass the first time. It was a girl in there that got caught while I was there. We went to court together this morning. She said the first time she got caught they gave her 30 days in the county."

"Thirty days in the county? Oh now you really shitting me. Bitch I would die doing 30 days in the county."

Mannnn, what was happening. On everything I love, the whole time we had been stealing I never really thought about the consequences. I was just thinking about the money. Did I even have anything to do once I got this so-called money I was chasing? This shit had my mind going man. I know 30 days wasn't the end of the world but going to jail or being in jail wasn't my cup of tea, ya feel meh?

I swear I needed to do some soul searching or whatever they call it, smdh. "Aye can somebody drop me off? I need a shower and just need to get in the bed. Didn't nobody tell my peoples right?"

"Fuck we gone call them for. We called your dude and got some money from him and we all put the rest together, which reminds me. We gon need that back sis andddddd, before you get to flipping we ain't talking bout right now. Just saying, we gone need them couple dollars back, love you boo." Tonya decided to drop Candy off cause she wanted to stop at the liquor store on her way back, so me and Dani stayed at my house. This was our first time really being by ourselves since we fought.

"Did it seem like Candy was trying to blame me for her going to jail?"

In my head I was thinking, *Wasn't candy just right here and y'all just had this discussion?*

"I mean it sounded like it at first, but eventually I think she ended up just mad at herself for real. You probably shouldn't take it personal due to the fact she just got out the joint." We both started laughing cause it sounded funny. Just getting out the joint. Lawd. "That shit crazy for real though. We gotta get another hustle. We be going in and outta these malls damn near 7 days a week then expect these folks to not recognize us. I ain't never going back in Beachwood my nigga, hell no."

"You do not gotta tell me twice. I'm bout to start doing some other shit too."

"Like what?" The way Dani said, *Like what,* I felt like she doubted me or something.

"Girl I don't know—something. I like to talk so much, maybe I need to be an actress or something like that. Maybe a pimp, maybe a hoe, I don't know. All's I do know is getting caught going to jail ain't the plan for sho."

By the time Tonya got back from the store with the liquor, Dani and I was so high we didn't even want nothing to drink. I told her the day was over and she told me to tell Dani to come down so she could drop her off. Whew chile I was too happy they was gone. I done had my house full of folks since the day before and I needed some peace of mind.

I'm sitting on my couch trying to figure out how my life got in this direction. *Did I not want better for myself? Was I a product of my own environment? Or was I just settling for nothing?* I think a lot of times people get comfortable doing less. Especially when most of the people around you enjoy doing less too. That's why they say surround yourself with people you wouldn't mind being like. If you hate your job, hate your life and you hate the house you live in, it's a strong possibility that you hate yourself too. If you want better you will do better.

Chapter 9

The whole Candy going to jail thing had me on some, *I need to find another way to get some new money* shit. I made a lot of money from boosting, but it was beginning to scare me. Yes, I wanted the money but no, I didn't want all the risk that came with it. Candy had been out of jail about two weeks now and I still hadn't been to the mall yet. A bitch was scared straight.

Tonya and Dani never stopped and the very next day after Candy was out she was right back at it. Money was getting real low and I knew I had to do something, but I was hoping for a miracle at that point. I even put a few job applications in at some local call center spots. I didn't have any experience, didn't have a high school diploma, and they better not even think about asking me to take a piss test. Me getting a good job wasn't looking too good. Now that I think about it, maybe I was depressed around that time. Black folk act like we don't get depressed. I think that's just the history of us. When things get tough dust yourself off and try again. I wanted so much more for my life, but didn't even know how to achieve it.

I think there are a lot of people in this world that want to do better and know they can do better but honestly don't even know where they should start. I'm sure it doesn't help either when you ask for help or tell people you want to do better and they can't really understand you cause they don't even want better for themselves. I felt something in me at that time, but didn't know how to get it out.

I sat around for days thinking of a new master plan. Since I was little I always kept a journal with me. If you know me you know I've always made to-do list since forever. I mean, as simple as 1) Go to the mall and make money, 2) Go sell that shit. No matter how big or small the mission was I tried to plan out my days daily. I use to always think that was a good habit to have, but right now I was sitting up in my room like Brandy thinking about some illegal shit. It was crazy that I couldn't come up with anything. I decided that I was just gon continue to steal and try to be as careful as possible.

All this stressing and thinking had my head spinning in circles. I was spending so much money on weed it was crazy. Guess I didn't notice it before cause I was making money daily. When you not making anything you start to see every penny you spend. I hit up my regular weed man and told him to pull up at my crib. I had about $25 to spare for some bud. When the he pulled up he asked could he use my bathroom. He was my nigga and all but I really didn't like people coming in my house. Maybe he would give me a fatter sack if when he came in he saw me in my little bitty-ass boyshorts. I ran to the door and let him in and of course soon as he came in he looked right at my shorts. Got 'eeeeem.

When he came out he sat down and asked me how much I wanted to spend.

"Well I only got about $25, but I need about $35 worth. Hook a sister up one time, damn." He was smiling, so I assumed he might could make that possible.

"How you gone hook me up?" I hate when you ask somebody for something and they ask you for something right back.

"What you want nigga?" I asked, in that cute girly way, trying to make sure I got that sack I wanted.

"How much some of that pussy going for?" I was stuck. Yeah yeah, I know I said I sold pussy, but I was lightweight lying. What I meant to say was, I would sell some pussy if it came down to it. I didn't mean I was willing and ready. This nigga had just asked me what it was going for and honestly, I couldn't even tell him. How much do you sell your most prize possession for? Ain't your coochie supposed to be the place you didn't let anyone in that didn't belong? A place only made for someone you love?

"I'll give you $200 and you don't have to pay for your sack."

Well damn. I'm sitting here stuck trying to figure out how much this thang was hitting for and he done threw a number out there with perks. I wondered could I have told him a higher price, but right then, right there, I wanted that lil soft $200 famlee.

"Okay."

He looked at me surprised like he couldn't believe I agreed to that shit.

"Did you just say okay?"

"Yes dude, now stop looking at me all crazy before I change my mind." He took off his coat and got comfortable.

Now look, I know what y'all thinking. You're probably thinking, *How could you stoop so low and you're so much better than that, blah blah blah*. This the way I see it though. If two people met each other and decided they wanted to sleep with each other, they would do just that. Rather it worked out or not they still would have slept together. In this situation it was the same thing only I'm getting some money and it's no strings attached. Was I scared, Uh yeahhh! But after a bitch ain't been to the mall in two weeks that $200 was sounding lovely.

He rolled up a blunt and we just sat there talking for a minute. It's crazy because all this time I been buying weed from this dude I never really found him attractive, or maybe I just wasn't paying attention to him. He was looking real good today though. Like a whole ass snack. Or did I just know he was bout to spend dem couple of dollars and that's what made him sexy? After we finished smoking he went in his pockets and counted me out $200 in 20's and threw it on the dresser. I sorta kinda just a little bit felt a little sleezy like, *Did he just throw my money on the dresser as if I was a prostitute or something,* but I wasn't tripping cause however you threw it up there don't matter long as it was there.

We was sitting in my front room at first, but after the money was exchanged I figured we should take it to my room. I was getting nervous now, I couldn't believe I was about to have sex with someone I only knew on a weed man and customer basis. It felt weird, like, *Was my pussy even gone get wet for a nigga I didn't even like?* By the time we made it to the room he was kissing all over me, grabbing all on my ass and shit. He was definitely getting me in the mood. He pushed me on the bed and started pulling my pants down, whole time still kissing all over my neck and shoulders. By the time he got to my panties I was so wet and ready for him to stick it in. It was clear that I hadn't got fucked in a while cause the weed man was about to get all this bidness. I'm purrrrring like a kitten waiting for him to stick it in and he spreads my legs apart and starts eating my pussy like it was his. Whoa, I did not know you get head too when people buy coochie. Didn't know that was a part of the package. "Got Damn!" Oh shit, did I just say that out loud? This dude was sucking my coochie so good I wanted to give him the money for my sack again. Give em a tip or something. "Whew!" I wanted him to stop cause it felt so good, but I also wanted him to keep going cause I was bout to bust. "Oh God, Oh, hmmmmmmm." Why did this dude just do me like that? That shit felt so good. I busted all in and on Mr. Weed man's face. He stood up and starting taking his clothes off. I'm laying there looking like a dead corpse just done. He got to his boxers and when he took them off I almost fainted. Okay Weed man. Imma just start calling him horsey. Right when I thought it couldn't get any better he whipped that sausage out. Listen, I ain't lied to y'all not one time yet and I'm not going to start now. Dude fucked the shit out of me period dot com. He had to be every bit of 6'4 and slim as shit. Y'all know what they say about them slim dudes, yup that they keep a long weenie and he fit the description perfect.

Prior to this encounter I had only had sex about five times and two of them times was with the same person so this was all new-new to me. I sat there watching him slide that condom on that long ass dick and I almost jumped up and ate that mu fucka. He got on top of me and starting sucking on my titties. I was moaning so loud I'm sure the neighbors heard me.

When he slid that dick up in me I wanted to tell him right then that I was his new trick bitch. How he had my coochie feeling I wanted to pay him but I wasn't crazy though. For some strange reason, I thought when niggas bought pussy it was real trashy and slutty. Nope, not with this guy. I felt like I was getting screwed by my husband.

Lately I just hadn't been in the mood for sex, but Mr. Weed man changed that shit up quick. Honestly, I didn't want it to stop. Shit felt simply amazing. We laid there for a minute just gathering our thoughts and our breath. He rolled over and asked me did I like it. My heart was beating fast, my coochie still throbbing from busting that enormous nut and he wanna ask me how it was.

"It was good."

Didn't wanna pump his head up and have em thinking that his dick was so good I didn't wanna get paid next time. Look at me, hoping it was a next time. Thirsty.

I wanted to tuck myself up under his arms and lay the fuck up, but I had to shake that off. He was just a trick and no matter how good the dick was I was not gon let him know that shit was fire. I hopped up and went and got him a rag. I usually only wiped my hoes down but since he had that magic dick he got the wipe me down special.

After I cleaned him up, we just laid there talking. He got to talking about how he wanted to make this a weekly thing and how he be trapping so hard he really ain't have time for a relationship, so he just be trying to get some pussy every now and then. It did NOT sound bad I'll tell you that. For one, I gets paid, whoot-whoot! And for two, I would love getting this package once a week. I'm laying in my bed with the weed man and I just had sold him some coochie. Wow. Was this for real? Had I done lost my damn mind?

Yes I talked about it and yes, I even thought about it, but this was really my first time selling a yam dinner and it was to the weed man. Ain't never even looked at him like that. Never even noticed that he was so cute. Only thing I did know was it felt good and we can do this every weekend if that was alright with him.

He got up and went and got the weed out of the other room. Sitting there watching him walk around my room naked as fuck was doing something to me. I wanted more of that. It took everything in me not to hop on his dick and ride that baby into the sunset, but I had to keep my cool vibe going at the time. I still couldn't believe I just sold my very first piece of ass. I thought I would feel gross afterwards, but what

I was feeling was definitely not gross. More like hornier than ever. I was in love. Lol, just kidding.

That's how females be though. Get some good dick and start calling him your man. Not to his face though just to your friends. Women know we some emotional characters and when you add dick into the equation we really get loopy.

When it was all said and done we smoked the rest of the blunt and he put all his clothes on and was ready to roll. He told me once again that he would love to do this more often and I told him that's cool with me. He made me out a nice lil sack, put it on the table next to my ends and rolled out. When the door shut, I screamed. Okay, okay, okay, okay, I gotta tell the homies Omg.

I called Tonya first and told her to pull up to the crib Neow. She like, *Is you okay?*

"Yes bitch I'm great, now get here." I couldn't wait to tell her bout this shit. I could still feel my legs shaking around this puppy.

So let me get this straight, I got paid to feel that good? Got paid to let a man suck on me like I was his own personal lolli pop. Where do I sign the yearly contract? I wondered could I make a living off selling pussy. My mind, body, and soul was all over the place that day. This guy had just come over and made me forget about anything else. I wanted to call him up and be like, *Heyyyyyyyyyyy, you wanna live together and do it every night?* But instead I just got cleaned up and starting straightening up the house. My life was crazy man. One crazy story after another. I couldn't wait to tell Tonya what had just went down. I mean maybe, just maybe, if I didn't feel like going to the mall everyday, I could just sell a lil coochie every now and then. I didn't want to make it official, but I think I had just put this pussy on the market. What the fuck!

Chapter 10

People always say when girls are in the streets or start using drugs it's always because they didn't have a father in the home or their mother was on crack. Well, here I stand before you. My mother wasn't on crack and I had a great father that, by the way, would've killed me if he knew what I was doing. Sometimes people just be lost and it has nothing to do with their parents.

Society is so hard on folks these days. I knew right from wrong, my parents didn't raise a fool and they damn sure didn't raise a hoe, but somewhere down the line a hoe was born. Now don't judge me, I was not proud of my actions, but mama had to pay them bills.

So listen here, after that encounter I had with my weed man I was ready to go-go.

To this day I will never tell you that I loved selling pussy, fuck naw. What I would say is I liked the money and sometimes it came with perks. After that first night I hooked up with dude I couldn't wait to tell my girls how that shit had went down. I was still thinking bout that nigga the next day like damn, where they do that at? I guess I just never expected paid sex to be so good. I thought when someone bought some pussy he dogged that shit and disrespected you. Maybe that was just in the movies. We all had been thinking about something else we could do so I was just gone shoot this out there.

One day one of our homegirls was having a baby shower, so I decided to chop it up with them there about my little fiesta. I was thirsty to give them all the deets. There's two kinds of freaks; one that likes to talk about what she does in the bedroom, and one that doesn't . I loved to. Them was my girls and I just had the kind of personality that liked to hear others opinions about different things—helped me understand the world more if you asked me.

I knew deep down I was gon be selling pussy. I was still gon be stealing too. I just thought that a little balance wouldn't hurt anybody. I just wanted to hear what the ladies had to say and was any of them down. Every female has a freak in her. It just takes the right situation or the right person to bring it out.

Today was gone be a good day I could feel it. I jumped up and opened up my curtains to let the sun in. Was it possible that I had a different pep in my step this morning? Had I found myself a new hustle and was ecstatic about the adventure? Was I elated that I had myself an extra $200 duckies this morning? Or was the real reason I was smiling and dancing and prancing around this morning was the fact that I got all that good long dick last night, yesss lawd. I felt embarrassed just thinking about it. If this how the business was gon be going I think I might get MVP at this job.

I hurried up and got dressed. I still needed to stop and get my girl a gift. I was 19 years-old and mostly everybody around us was having babies. I mean from the girls who was fast to the girls that was tomboys, everybody was pregnant. That was a trend I wasn't trying to be down with. I couldn't even see myself with a baby daddy right now. I looked at all niggas like they was all immature and not really worth my time. At 19, girls should be thinking about traveling the world and finding out who they was, not chasing behind somebody's dumb ass son and carrying a baby around. Anyways I got all my shit together and headed to Target to get something for this baby shower. I always went with diapers because a new mom-to-be could never have enough and babies was always shitting everywhere.

Tonya text me saying she had just pulled up and I told her I was 20 minutes away. She like, *Hurry up bitch I'm ready to hear this new money making plan you done came up with.* Was she really ready to hear it though. I wondered was the girls gon think I was crazy as fuck for even thinking this was a plan B. None of them came up with one so I was gon shoot my shot. Rather or not the girls was down I was still gon do me. Me, Dani and Candy all pulled up around the same time. Ever since Candy had caught that case she had been moping around these last couple of days. I know that shit had to be frustrating thinking about having a case pending, especially when you didn't even really know what to expect.

We had been asking everybody we knew who caught a case at Beachwood what to expect and all of them said the exact same thing. She was going to jail.

We all walked into the baby shower together. Tonya already had us a table in the back. We was all too ghetto to be posted up somewhere in the front. You have to put the petty people in the back so they laughs and giggles could go unnoticed. Soon as I sat down I see we all was thinking the same thing. Diapers. "So we all just gone come with diapers though, we ain't shit!" They had just started making plates so I was right on time. I hated coming to baby showers after everybody ate. Food be all cold and nasty by then and everybody be looking at you eat your lil leftovers. We were all sitting there laughing and eating, and Dani like, "Sooo, hello, don't you have some big news you wanted to drop on us, whats good?"

"I mean I wouldn't say its some big news, I just said yesterday I made $200 pretty quick and I thought we all might could use a few extra dollars."

"Spit that shit out hoe," Tonya said, while stuffing her face with somebody's pasta salad.

" Okay listen up now, I know y'all probably gon think I'm crazy, but just here me out first." They all was eating, but they all was looking and listening hard as fuck. All eyes was on me. Bet.

"Okay so yesterday I was about to get some weed from Big Mike and things went a little different than I thought. In the middle of him making my sack he asked me how much I charged for some pussy." Tonya almost spit her food out: "What!"

"Yes bitch, while he was putting my shit on the scale just busted out of nowhere and said he had $200 to fuck." They were no longer eating shit. Mouths was wide open looking shocked. "He asked me how much and I didn't even know how much to tell him. He told me $200. So yup we fucked for the $200 and that shit was good as fuck."

"Hold up," Dani said. "So you telling me you fucked fine ass Big Mike yesterday for $200? She was trying to make sure she had all this right. "For $200," I told her. "He ate the fuck out of my pussy and fucked me like I was his bitch. We smoked a blunt after it was over and he left. The whole thing had to last every bit of 30 to 40 minutes."

Tonya, Dani and Candy were all just sitting there looking at me like I was crazy.

"So this the big money plan you was talking bout and saying we all should get with? From the way Candy was talking with all that sarcasm, I was assuming she wasn't down with the plan.

"Well I wasn't saying or trying to make anybody pop that thang open for a real nigga, I was just saying what I did and that I wouldn't have a problem doing it again. That was the quickest $200 I had ever made and it helped that Big Mike dicked me down so good. I didn't even have to leave my house to make that money."

"I don't know about all that Stoney. I got a nigga and I'm not sure how he's going to feel knowing his bitch was out here selling pussy." Most days I forgot that Candy even had a boyfriend. The way she hustled you would have never known. Ain't no way I'd have a nigga and still be out here asking other niggas for shit. But I felt her. If I had a nigga though, I wouldn't even have to think about shit like this, but maybe that was just me.

"Look I wasn't trying to force y'all into doing anything. All I was saying was making that $200 yesterday was a lick to me. I hadn't got fucked in a while too, so it was a win for me all the way around the board. I'm not trying to go to jail, so I been trying to chill a little on the mall. That don't mean I'm gone sell pussy full time. I just think having a few regulars won't hurt anybody, especially if they coming through like Big Mike did.

"Out of nowhere Dani like, "I'm down." We all looked over at her like, huh?

"Wait did I just hear you clearly? Did you say you was down to sell that lil pocketbook bitch?"

"Look I'm trying to move out my mama's house and a whole bunch of other shit, so I need all the extra money I can get. We will fuck a nigga for free in a heartbeat so why not make a couple dollas. My grandma even told me to sell ass?"

"Wait a damn minute now you talking crazy, ain't nobody's grandma told them to sell some ass chile."

"Well to be exact, what she said was, shouldn't no woman be walking around broke when she was sitting on a golden ticket." Some ole' Willy Wonka and the Chocolate Factory-ass riddle. Moral of the story was, You better make that mu-fucka do what it do.

We sat there cracking up about all kinda shit the whole shower. If I wouldn't have had any cake I would not have even thought we went to the shower. We acted like it was just us there. From the way it sounded Dani was in, but Candy and Tonya wasn't. Its not like I was trying to force people to sell no ass. I was just looking for another way to bring in some money. I think that's why when you surround yourself with people you got to make sure everyone has a good brain on their shoulders, so we all can be thinking about a master plan. This was the only thing I came up with but I was the only one that came up with anything, I didn't hear no other get-money plans at the table.

Maybe mine wasn't the smartest, but at least I had one. Use what you got to get what you want. I think that was how the saying went.

I'm glad I wasn't by myself though. Dani was feeling me. She might not have been feeling the plan that much, but she was willing to see what was up. She was a freak, so I think she liked the sex part more than the money. Dani probably was already fucking a few niggas at that moment and I'm positive she wasn't getting a penny from none of them. It's crazy cause to this day Dani always says I'm the reason she got started doing that and if it wasn't for me she would have never even started selling pussy. Hey, hey, hey now, don't blame me for that. You and your pussy has a mind of they own. Don't blame me.

Chapter 11

Things had become different with the crew lately. Not different in a bad way, just different. Everybody was just doing they own thing which was good. We all were still in the malls but mentally we was in two different worlds.

I think when Dani and me started our new hustle, that bridged a gap between us and Tonya and Candy. No one never said anything, but I always felt like they judged us. I mean, we was all committing sins if you asked me and one ain't no different from the other. I never held that against them, they would always be my sisters no matter what.

Dani had really got comfortable with the tricking aspect of things. She barely even went to the malls anymore. I was still doing both. I had a few regulars, but I went and got most of my money from them stores. Every trick was not like Big Mike I tell you. What I pictured and how I started was not the way things really went. Men definitely felt that if they was paying you they could treat you however they wanted as long as they was paying. It went from, I could do this forever to, I hope this nigga not trying to hook up tonight. The more I hooked up with different men the more I felt bad about myself. I didn't enjoy any of it anymore.

It even started making me hate men in general. I would hook up with married men and they would spend a majority of the time talking about how much their wives got on their nerves. I use to sit there and wonder if I ever got married would my husband be somewhere paying for pussy, talking shit about me? It was just a really bad time for me. It was also a good time though, because it made me question myself and how I got to that point. My life had somehow only revolved around money and getting it. I wasn't going to family functions, I barely went out to party with friends, and my dating life was non-existent, because in my mind I thought, who would want to date a girl who's a trick? I remember it was days I would just lay in the bed the whole day just depressed. I didn't like who I had become and I wanted to change so much but just didn't know how. Ever been in that place? You wanna do better, but just don't know the first step to take. I had plenty conversations with the homies, but they weren't hearing me. Dani had fell in love with selling pussy, I mean like, that really was her thing. She loved the attention and everything else that came with it. Tonya and Candy was addicted to hustling and had no plans on stopping. It wasn't even about the hustle at that point. They loved the thrill of going in and out of the malls and the adrenaline rush they got every time they almost got caught. That Beachwood case that Candy had came and went. They made her do 10 days in the county jail, pay a fine of $500 dollars and the case was finished. She knocked those 10 days out so quick we barely knew she was gone.

You would think that after she did them days it would have slowed her down. Nope, she was actually going harder. Honestly, at that point in my life I just wanted to live a regular life. I wanted a regular job, a regular boyfriend and anything else that was just a part of being regular.

Around this time, Dani had started dating this dude named Randy. I don't know if I should even say *dating* Randy. Randy was a trick both

Dani and me had hooked up with a few times. She just actually started liking dude. I never understood how she would fall for these tricks. If a nigga was buying pussy from me ain't no telling who else he buying it from. Not to mention, how you even take a nigga serious who's a trick. Anyhoo, she was really feeling dude and at this time since she had fallen for him I stopped answering his calls.

One day I go to meet her to get some shoes I had left in her trunk and he was in the car with her. I said what's up and told her to pop the trunk so I could get my stuff. Here come Randy talking bout do I need any help. I'm like, Naw I'm good. I could see Dani looking in her rear view mirror trying to see what was going on. Oh nothing, just this nigga you loving trying to see if I was trying to hook up with him again. I told him I was cool, got my shoes, hopped back in my whip and rolled out. Later, that night I got a call from Dani saying she was in my neighborhood and wanted to stop by and blow one with me. That was perfect cause I had come home with no weed and wasn't none of the weed men answering.

We sitting there smoking, watching some reality TV bullshit I had on the tube when Dani asks me when was the last time I hooked up with Randy. I know this bitch ain't got me out of my bed to come ask me some stupid ass questions about a tricking ass nigga that clearly was checking for me.

"Girl I ain't hooked up with that nigga in about two months, please don't worry yourself boo-boo" The nerve of this hoe.

"Oh I wasn't worried I just saw y'all talking and you was all giggling and shit, it looked like y'all might've still had something going on and I just wanted to know cause he stay on my heels.

"Girl if you came over here to question me about Randy trick ass you gone blow my whole entire high. Don't nobody want his ass but you. I been stopped answering his phone calls and text, take care." She got to saying how she wasn't tripping and how he wasn't her man and blah blah blah. I was barely even paying her any attention. I was trying to finish that blunt off and get my ass back in the bed and that's exactly what I did—we smoked, she left and I got my ass in the bed. She came over here to see if I was checking for Randy when I was the last person she needed to be worried bout. He had all kinda hoes and she was just one of them. Girl goodbye.

If you know anything about a thirsty nigga you know they will try anything to get your attention. First thing the next morning here go my phone ringing bright and early. It was Randy, and of course, I didn't answer. He called me about three times back to back and I started to just pick the phone up and cuss his silly ass the fuck out, but that probably would've made him even more happier so I just hit ignore. You would think after I didn't pick up he would give up, but not Mr. Thirsty man himself. I looks down at my phone only to see I had three missed text messages as well. I wanted to call Dani and tell her come get her man out my phone, but she would've hopped right in her feelings I'm sure. I open up the message and the first thing I see is, *Why you tell Dani?* I picked up the phone and called him back. "Why I tell Dani what?" I wasn't never bout to go back and forth with no text, but I damn sure wanted to know what I told Dani." You can tell by how he answered the phone that he was on some trash.

"Why you tell Dani that you been stopped fucking with me and you blocked me and all that other corny shit?" I know this girl ain't went back and told this man all these lies just to throw me under the bus like I gave a fuck.

"Negro I ain't even tell her that. I told her I stopped answering your calls, that's it. The only reason I did that was because I knew y'all had whatever y'all had going on. That was corny as fuck of her to tell you that. What you want though?" Hoes do the corniest things for a nigga. He already a trick, but you wanna try to make me look bad like I'm talking to you bout him when here he go still over here checking for me. You big dummy!

"Girl I don't even care what you said, I just wanna see you again," he said over the phone. Me and Dani ain't shit but friends, just like me and you. I know you need a couple dollars. Let me slide through real quick." That's what he would've loved to do. Nigga you been all up under my girl telling her plenty of lies and now you wanted to come spend ya lil coins over here? That's why I didn't take none of them serious. People always be like, Stoney why you don't got a nigga. I be looking at them like, Cause I don't wanna be sitting somewhere loving somebody who didn't even respect me. I was good on all that.

"Yeah I'm cool B. I don't have no time to be getting into it with Dani about you. The money not even worth the drama. She done already questioned me about you, then went back and told you a million lies for what I have no idea, yeah I'm tight on that shit. It was good talking to you, ba-bye." I hung up that phone so quick.

Men be the biggest shit starters. I'm sure him and Dani done had plenty conversations about me, now all of a sudden you wanna call me about it. Niggas will sit up and listen to you talk dirty as hell about a bitch, agree with all the shit you saying, call her out of her name, then the minute you not around go look for that bitch. And us women fall for the goofy shit all the time. There's no way I would even be taking this nigga serious knowing that me and my girl tricked with him.

I wasn't gon call Dani at first. I was just gon act like I never talked to him and let her continue to look stupid, but the pettiness in me called her anyway. Sometimes you have to call corny people out on the hoe shit they be doing cause sometimes they don't even be knowing they doing it. I like to give some people the benefit of doubt but Dani knew better. She was just acting like a weak ass hoe.

She answered the phone all chipper like everything was everything, you know that fake shit people be doing.

"What did you tell Randy I said about him." I wasn't bout to play no games with her ass. She was quiet for a minute then she like, "What is you talking about?" I learned from checking many bitches in my lifetime that when a bitch say, "What is you talking about," she usually knows exactly what you talking about. "Girl don't play dumb now. You told him I was calling him thirsty and I told you I told him not to call me no more and a bunch of shit I didn't say. I'm trying to figure out why you felt the need to tell this nigga anything especially when he then comes back and tells me everything you said. That shit was corny as fuck Dani." Cat must've not only had her tongue but he also had her brain too, cause after I said all that, the only thing she could come up with was she ain't never said no shit like that to him and he lying and why would she tell him that stuff. Luckily we was on the phone cause right about now she deserved to be smacked in the mouth. Bitch knew damn well she told that nigga all that stuff. Shit like that made me wanna stop fucking with females period.

If I'm being corny somewhere pillow talking and somebody ask me about it I'm just gone admit I was being corny. Playas fuck up too, you know. I'm not gone sit up and lie and make myself look completely silly then.

"So you didn't say nothing at all about me to Randy? I just got off the phone with him and he told me everything you said. So he lying then?"

"Girl that nigga just wanna fuck, so he trying to tell you anything to get it."

"But he don't have to tell me anything, he done bought some pussy from me before so he know all he gotta say is he got some money for me. What would he get out of making this all up?" I could not believe Dani was just sitting up lying over some weak-ass shit like this. It wasn't even that serious. We all knew she was loving this nigga so why not just say that. "Look that nigga thirsty," Dani said, "and he trying to put me in it I guess, I don't know, but I ain't said shit to him. I'm trying to figure out why y'all was laying up discussing me anyways." Was this bitch delusional? When thee fuck did I say we was laying up anywhere! See, her mind was playing tricks on her cause she was in her feelings heavy.

"Laying up! Girl that nigga ain't touched me in months. I said he called me, but clearly you didn't hear that at all."

"Girl you funny. You like that nigga Randy and that's why you told him all that shit. Can't even be a real bitch and say you said it." Ain't nobody thinking bout him but you and he got you looking stupid as fuck running back telling me what yo pillow-talking ass was saying. You corny as fuck Dani, but you already know that." I hung up on that hoe before I said something I couldn't take back. I wasn't about to sit on the phone listening to her act like she ain't said shit and she ain't know what the fuck was going on. I swear, I was getting so tired of going through bullshit with my friends. I thought you was supposed to grow old with the people you grew up with. Baby if this was what my future was looking like it was time to start making some changes ASAP. I woke up the next day with a clear mind and more fully focused on making some changes in my life. Fucked up though because that day was the day I caught my first felony. Guess that wasn't the change

I was looking for.

Chapter 12

No lie, once you catch one case you become a magnet for bullshit. I went from not having any cases, to three in one year. I was hottttttt! Crazy thing is, every time I got caught I swear it was because of somebody else being hot and shit.

I was grabbing lawyers sometimes or if they appointed me a good public defender I'd roll with him. I think for like 2-3 years straight I was on probation. I would catch a case in some off-brand city and they would bond me over to the county, thirsty to try and give me a felony. It's crazy because back then people talked about a felony like it was the worst thing in the world. Ohhh, you have a felony you'll never amount to anything. No one will hire you. You won't be able to find a good placc to stay. Paleaseeee do not believe that shit. You can do whatever you apply yourself to do. I know people without felonies that ain't shit, ain't gon never be shit, and they daddies probably wasn't shit either. It's really all up to you what you do with your life.

I started getting them left and fucking right though, like, who does that? I'm fighting these cases as hard as I could, but I always ended up pleading to some Receiving Stolen Property shit, which ended up being a big fat felony 5. I still didn't understand that charge. Exactly what did I receive? I stole it myself, duh. Just thinking about it makes me mad because when you're young and going to court, most of the times you don't even be knowing what them judges and prosecutors be talking about and they know that. Half the time the parents don't be knowing either and that's why we have so many juveniles locked up. The justice system is a bad mu-fucka and I was pissed because that was my new life. Growing up as a kid you never think you're life will end up tangled in the court system. Especially as a woman. I guess all good things have to come to an end and this lifestyle had landed me in the county jail, headed to prison.

"Smith! Smith!! Get your stuff, it's time to ride out."

I thought I was dreaming, but if it was, this would definitely be a nightmare. I kept hearing my name being called, but it felt like I couldn't get up and open my eyes. Maybe I didn't wanna get up and open my eyes. I knew they said I would be riding out soon, but I damn sure wasn't in no rush to get to prison.

All the ladies in the county jail with me kept trying to tell me all about it. What to do, what not to do. I wasn't really scared cause I knew I could hold my own, it was just the fact that I was about to be in prison with killers and rapist and all kind of shit I see on the local news every night. I really couldn't believe this was now my life.

I finally opened my eyes and started getting all my belongings. I knew I would be heading to prison soon so on the last commissary day I ordered enough personals that would last me until I got settled in. Not like I would ever truly get settled in.

It was another girl they had woke up who I could see was up getting ready too. I was glad of that because I was starting to really get nervous. The CO's was rushing us so I just rolled all my shit up in a sheet and headed to the door to wait for the other chick. She looked like she could possibly be my age but them drugs had her looking all fucked up. This was her fourth time going to Marysville--the women's prison in Ohio they send all the females to. This was gon be my first and my last time you can bet that.

As we walked towards the elevator I saw other women coming from their pods holding their shit in they hands. Guess we all was headed to hell that morning. We all got on the elevator and the CO told us to face the back. As an inmate you get treated like shit. They talk down on you all day, look at you like you killed somebody even when you just there for Check Fraud or some shit. It's just a very humiliating place. I know its not supposed to be Disney fucking World, but we're still humans.

They put us all in a room and told us we would be leaving out shortly. The closer and closer I got to actually going to that place, the more my head started to hurt. When you go to prison they give you your clothes you came in with to wear down there. They not about to let you take them county blues up outta there. I didn't even remember what I had on when I came in. As they gave us our belongings and told us to get dressed, you could clearly see what folks was on when they got booked in. The white girl I said came down with me was most definitely a prostitute, ha. She had on a short-ass mini-skirt, some fishnets and a half top. Somebody was working-working before she got picked up.

I put on my clothes and looked in the mirror. All I could do was shake my head. I had let myself down at this point.

From the looks of things I was going to jail with a few crackheads, a few prostitutes, a few heroin addicts, and this one white, fancy lady that looked like she worked for the president or some shit. I wonder what she did to be headed to prison. Guess who wasn't bout to ask her though? In my heart I knew I wasn't bout to do them whole 3 years, I just couldn't. I didn't know how I was gon do it, but there was no way I could. No way I could be away from my son that long.

I was keeping it together because I didn't want to look like a bitch, but deep down I was still sick to my stomach.

When they started loading us on the bus my heart was beating fast as ever cause I knew this was really it. They piled us all in like sardines and we rode out. It was a two-hour drive from the County to Marysville, but it was the longest two hours ever. I had so much running through my head on that ride. I sat there the whole time looking out the window just reflecting on my life. Who would've ever thought I'd be on my way to the big house, the slammer, the joint, the grown-up punishment, the whatever you want to call it. All the other ladies sat on the bus having different conversations, but every time one of them would even begin to say anything to me I would just give em that evil eye like don't fucking talk to me.

I wasn't happy about going to prison. I didn't want to make jokes and talk about our lives on the streets. I wanted to go home to my house, to my bed, to my kid. I sat on the bus the whole drive there, quiet as a church mouse. I just stared out the window the entire time.

When we finally pulled up I was in shock of how the place looked more like a college dorm area than a prison. Oh, don't get me wrong, bob wire was wrapped all around that baby, so it was for sure a prison. But it looked much different than I expected it to. As we was rolling through headed to the back all you could see was a bunch of women walking around the yard. I could not believe my eyes. Everybody was just walking around smiling and shit like this wasn't prison. My mouth was wide open as I stared at all the ladies. So many pretty faces and smiles all locked up behind bars. What in the world did all these women do to end up here?

I saw old-ass white women and young beautiful black girls all just going about their way. Everybody was looking at us as we rode in, waving and looking to see who the newcomers were. The whole ride I sat slumped down in my seat but now I was sitting straight up, amazed at the sight. So many beautiful women were there living life, doing their time.

I was still gazing out the window when I felt the bus come to a stop. I couldn't see any women anymore, just a big, ugly building that looked like it had been there since this place opened. It had moss all over it and the windows were all covered in bars. Did the pretty women I just saw live here or was this where the ugly girls lived or some shit? It looked like a dungeon and we was pulling up straight to that baby. I heard the door slam and when I looked up it was some big dikey-looking woman walking out headed towards us. She came to the bus looking like she was about to be on some bullshit.

"Listen we can have a good day or a bad day, it's all up to you," she barked. "I need everybody to keep their mouths shut so we can get this process done and over with as quick as possible. Once we get inside, all of you are going to one room where you will wait for your name to be called and we'll go from there. There is to be no talking."

This lady's whole face was red and all she was doing was talking. You could tell she was racist by the tone of her voice. We all got up one by one and started walking into the building. They started taking off our shackles once we got to the entrance. I took my first step in the building and could feel my heart beating like fuck. It was so crazy because the first person I seen was an inmate and she was giving us a change of clothes. After that, I noticed everybody that worked over where we were was inmates. They gave us our clothes, explained our inmate handbooks, and everything else we did. The state gets all that money for each inmate that comes in them doors and they got the inmates doing all the work. The few correctional officers that WAS working, was sitting there stuffing their faces and looking at us like we was the worst people on earth. I don't think I have ever felt as low as I felt when I walked through them doors. The way they treat you when you're in prison is some other kinda shit.

We all sat in one room waiting for our names to be called. We couldn't go to the bathroom, couldn't talk, couldn't ask questions, nothing. They told us to just sit there and wait while they took they sweet 'ole time getting to us. After about an hour of sitting in that little ass room with all them funky ass women they started calling our names. It's like they went from slow to Speedy Gonzalez. "Smith let's go!" some lady shouted. I jumped up and went over to her. She took me to a room and told me to strip ass-hole naked. I told her it was that time of the month and asked could I just leave my panties on since I had a maxi-pad on. She yelled so damn loud I flinched. "I said take everything off including your panties! Throw the pad away and stand straight up in front of me." I felt soooooo disgusting man.

The way the CO's treat you in prison makes no sense. Not saying they supposed to treat us like royalty, but they definitely take their jobs a bit overboard. She had me cough and squat a few times as she did a complete body search. I had my eyes closed most of the time and was trying to fight back the tears filling up in my eyes. If that wasn't humiliating enough, she then told me to head towards the shower. She gave me some sort of shampoo she said would make sure I didn't have lice. Told me to put it on any part of my body that had hair on it. I was freezing like hell but I quickly put the crappy shampoo all over my body. When I went to wash it all off, the water was freezing fucking cold. Wowwwwwww. I rinsed that shit off quick as fuck an got up outta there.

From there they gave me some kind of moo-moo and told me to

step in the next room. You would think because the CO's was ladies they would have some sorta understanding, but naw they ain't give a damn.

When I went to the other room, a doctor was there. She told me to get on the table and lay down. Everything they did was aggressive. I had plenty of pap-smears before, but this doctor was so rough it damn near felt like rape. A tear rolled down my eyes while it was happening. I just couldn't believe that stealing some shit from the mall could send me here to get mistreated like this. I felt like an animal.

Once that was over they sent me to yet another room where it was a few other girls from the ride sitting down. I hadn't talked to none of them hoes much, but now I was eager to ask them about the way we was being treated.

"Yoooo was that doctor aggressive or what?" Everybody just sat there quiet as fuck like they didn't hear me. "Y'all okay?" These bitches was yapping all the way down, now they wanna be on mute. One of the white girls looked at me then looked out of the room then whispered, "Girl, just don't say shit 'til it's over or they'll make it even worse." *Worse! How could this shit get worse?* is what I was thinking, but I shut the fuck up cause I didn't want to find out. That was my first day in prison and it just kept going downhill from there.

After we had been bounced around from room to room they finally told us after about 5 hours that they were going to take us out to where we would be sleeping at for the next 40 days. We all followed the CO through the yard. We walked past a few different buildings, but most of them looked like they wasn't in use no more. When we got to this one building the CO stopped and said this was our new home. It had *Hale* written on the front of the building. It should've been spelled like Hell cause that's exactly what it was.

I didn't see all those pretty women I saw walking through the yard any more. What I saw now was a big ass dorm with about 300-400 bunk beds and it was loud as fuck. Women was running around chasing each other, some was holding hands and some was there that didn't even look like women, then there was a group that looked like they was coming off every drug in the world. This didn't look like prison, it looked like a zoo and I was mad as fuck that this was my new home. Fuck my life.

Chapter 13

They sat us all in what they called "The Dayroom" to quickly explain the rules and regulations of Hale Cottage and then threw us to the wolves. I mean like, *Hey ladies, welcome to Hale. I don't want no shit outta you so watch yourself, now go find your bed.* Excuse me? Bitch you better introduce me to a few bitches real quick or something. Tell me where the bathrooms at, what time I can use the phone, something!!! Everybody just starting walking to they assigned beds.

I picked my lil net bag of belongings and walked to find my bed too. It felt like everybody was staring at me. I was trying not to look nervous and scared, but I was frightened. All that tough shit I was talking done went out the window. This place smelled like piss and it seemed like nobody cared. That was a big problem for me. Like how is all these people chilling in this place and it stank like urine?

I finally found my bed and it was a little bitty black old lady sitting on it. Old school didn't even give me a chance to put my shit down before she started telling me bout this so-called living area.

"Look we bunkies and it's some shit you need to know," she said, looking up at me. "I don't like people over here by my shit, so if you got any lil girlfriends keep em away from over here. Don't ask me for nothing cause I'm not here to take care of nobody but myself. And last but not least, keep all your shit on your side of the bed, okay? I wanted to tell this old bitch get your California raisin-looking-ass outta my face before I smacked her ass into the dayroom, but I kept it cute.

"Well first of all, I don't fuck with girls so it won't be no girlfriend shit going on. I got my own shit, so I don't need shit from you and I plan on keeping all my shit on my bed so you can have both sides of this bitch if you want, how bout that?" She started smiling and I think that's how I met my first prison friend.

She had to be about 68, but she was cool as fuck, on everything. She showed me how to make my bed and where to hang my stuff at. Gave me the phone schedule and told me what times the shower actually be hot. After everything was put up and my bed was tightly made, I just sat there a moment looking around. Sooooo many women in prison for soooo many things. Shit was so sad to me cause I just kept thinking that so many of them was mothers too. So many of them felt just like me inside. Sick!! We were all adjusting to a new way of living temporarily, but our families didn't have a choice to adjust. Us coming to jail didn't just inconvenience ourselves, it's a huge inconvenience for the families left to take care of the responsibilities they didn't even ask for. I just sat there soaking it all in for a minute, because I really couldn't believe my eyes.

I'm sitting there just looking around when this lady who slept directly across from me fell out of her bed and started foaming at the mouth. No lie, I couldn't believe my freaking eyes! Everybody started yelling for the CO's and screaming, but not one of them came over there. I even thought I saw one look and turn around. I hopped off my bunk and ran over to the lady trying to see what I could do to help. As I was trying to pick her up I felt somebody grabbing all on my shoulders. I turned around and it was my old ass bunky. "Get your ass back on your bunk or you will regret it big time"

"BUT."

"But nothing, when them CO's come over here and see you trying to help her they will send your ass to the hole for being out of place. Now get the fuck back on your bed, I'm telling you this for your own good."

I was so lost like, How could all these people just sit there and watch this woman have a seizure and not do anything? I looked around and noticed wasn't nobody off their bunks. They was all screaming for help from their beds and they was all looking at me like I was crazy. I heard some walkie talkies and I hurried up and jumped back on my bed. A few CO'S and the nurse came walking down the aisle to where the women was. She was still laying on the floor shaking. They gave her a shot in her arm and literally threw her on a stretcher and rolled her out. I was speechless. They cared for her like her life didn't mean anything. This was a cold place and I hadn't even seen the worst.

That night I cried myself to sleep with my head under the covers so no one could see me. They say you don't truly find yourself until you hit rockbottom. Well this was my bottom. This had to be the lowest I had ever been. I was in a room with about 350 women that was there for who knows what and we were under the supervision of people who didn't give a complete fuck about any of us. It couldn't get any lower than that. Hopefully.

Chapter 14

You know what I found out after talking to a lot of those women in there? My childhood wasn't so bad after all. Some of the stories I heard from those women was horrible.

Your first 30 days in prison is for you to learn the rules and regulations of the place--what to do, what not to do, what areas you should and should not be in and them kinds of things. They also make you go through weeks of these classes that cover shit from addiction to abuse. I think the classes were set in place to show you how you and a lot of these women had more in common than you knew.

I remember one class I was in the instructor asked the group, "If you never been molested raise your hand." Let me repeat that for you. She said if you NEVER been molested raise your hands. I looked around a room of maybe 150 people or so and only me and about 10 ladies raised their hands. I couldn't believe my eyes. To look around and see that only 10 people out of 150 had never been molested was crazy. I started thinking like, *Damn. A lot of these women had the odds stacked against them early.*

Prison is supposed to be this place where you get some kind of rehabilitation, but most of the times due to the system being so fucked up, that never happens. I don't know about rehabilitation, but I started looking at the world differently. I sorta stopped being so judgmental after meeting so many women who had a helluva story to tell. I tried not to get too friendly with too many people, but most of the women I met was sweet as pie.

I remember I met this one chic from Dayton. Her story was so crazy I still remember all the details to this day. She said it was on Easter Sunday when she caught her case. Her and her family was headed to church. She had just finished getting her kids dressed when she heard somebody banging on the door. When she went to answer it she realized it was her exes baby mama. The girl was irate and screaming all kinda bullshit about beating her ass and she took her man. She told her kids to get away from the door and went out to talk to the lady. They exchanged words and she told the woman to get off her property. After going back and forth, the baby mama started walking up on her porch trying to fight her. My friend pushed the lady out of her way and when the lady fell back she hit her head on a small rock that was in the driveway and died. Can you believe that shit???? She died immediately and even though the woman came to her house on bullshit they gave this girl 16 years for Manslaughter and 2nd degree Murder. Her story blew my mind and she told me that shit while we was waiting to go see the OBGYN. So you trying to tell me that if a bitch come to my house on trash and I defend myself and shit go wrong I could possibly spend the rest of my life in jail? Oh hell to the fuck naw. From now on, anybody that got a problem with me they got a problem with the police and you can call me a snitch or whatever. This was not the place you wanted to be.

The even crazier thing about her story was she was one of the nicest women I ever met. This lady had 4 children under the age of 13 and was doing a 16-year bid because someone came to her house on trash on Easter. Wow was all I could say.

Then there was Ms. Nita, who was serving a Life sentence because she just happened to go home early after a long day working at the hospital. She was a registered nurse and had two kids--a boy and a girl. She got home earlier than usual only to come home to find her boyfriend raping her 9-year old daughter. She then grabbed a vase off her dining room table and beat him to death. They charged her with murder and sent her to jail for life. Really? Who wouldn't do the same thing? I can't even imagine what was going through her head, but I know my actions would've been the same. Did y'all know that more than half of the women in prison is in there for something that involves a man? Example.

A lot of women are in jail for killing men who were abusive to them. There are also a lot of women in jail for taking the rap for niggas, like a man will rob a bank and have his woman with him or some way be a part of the situation and now she's an accessory. The stories I was hearing was fucked up and to listen to the women speak about them just brought tears to my eyes because their lives was over. Killed a nigga for raping your daughter and now you're in prison and someone else has to raise her which leaves her unprotected again. Hearing all these stories had me fucked up and looking at life a different way.

I think when you're sent to prison it's supposed to be for rehabilitation, but very seldom does that happen. People go to jail for one thing and learn a million other crimes while they're in there. The real reason is because the judge, the prosecutor, and society all want you to learn a lesson. That definitely was happening now. I went in thinking I was gon get raped or something crazy like that. Maybe I had watched wayyyy too many jail documentaries. Now I was feeling like maybe a few of these women could just really use a hug. Those first ten days of admissions was crazy. Everyday I met a new woman with a different story.

Don't get it confused, it was some women that damned sure deserved to be there, but they probably had one helluva story behind them too. My bunky was some old ass lady from Toledo who was like a Kingpin or some shit. We would sit up for hours all night long talking about some of everything. Every night before they turned the lights off this lady that slept right across from me would sing that Sam Cooke song, *A Change Gone Come.* It was wild because no matter how chaotic that place use to get whenever it was nighttime and the lights got low, people would be calm. They would read or whisper or whatever they did to relax, but the whole building would be still. It was like our reflection time. The time you took to just talk to yourself or God. Well that's what I used that time for. I always heard the saying, *Do your time don't let the time do you,* but now I really understood it. It's like all those women were there for different reasons and they all had different amounts of time so however you chose to get through it was completely up to that individual.

My plan, I thought, was to get down there mind my business, and get the fuck back home. But clearly plans was meant to be broken. I hadn't even planned on talking to half of those women, yet all of a sudden it seemed like it was only 10 days in and I'd heard so many stories I felt obligated to hear more.

I can remember sitting up on my bed one night just looking around. There were women sneaking to the bathrooms to have sex with their girlfriends, women up late exercising, women who just sat up all day and all night crying. Oh, and I cannot forget the loud snoring mu-fuckas that sounded like fucking bears, including my gangsta ass bunky. And then there was me, just trying to make sense of it all. I was young and even though I was in prison for stealing, I felt like I was there for some other reason. That's just the kind of person I was. Even when things were going bad I would always see the good in a situation.

Some people might say, *How in the hell can you see the good in prison?* I get that, but maybe I wasn't looking for the good in being in prison, maybe I was looking for the good in those women. When I started thinking like that my time just started to fly by and that was a good thing. I spent those next 20 days of admissions just talking to any and everybody that wanted to listen. People would say stuff like, "That woman killed her husband, stay away from her," but those are the people I would make sure I spoke to daily just to see what kind of energy they was giving off. Always pleasant just like I expected. It got to the point where people started looking for me just to talk.

I became the ears of Admissions which I thought was crazy, but whatever. Like I said for about 45 days, all of us 300 women stayed in the same dorm. We showered together, ate together, watched TV together, and we all went through our "Welcome to Marysville" programs together. To me, this felt more like camp than anything, but I guess after you realize you're sleeping next to killers and shit, that camp shit goes out the window.

I remember the first time we all cried together too. There was this lady who sorta was like the funny girl of the pod. She kept everybody laughing and in good spirits. I believe her name was Annette. She was in prison for writing bad checks or some kind of white collar crime. We use to all get our mail first thing in the morning at 5am, which I thought was completely crazy. They would make you get up early as fuck just to stand in a line and wait to see if your name was called. Bitch be mad as fuck after waiting all that time and you ain't get shit.

I remember Annette got a letter from home telling her to please call home ASAP. She kept trying to call, but no one was answering. She kept telling all of us how worried she was and we kept telling her that everything was fine. Everything wasn't fine though. Later that afternoon the Chaplain came in looking for. I believe she was out smoking or something, can't really remember. What I do remember was when they finally found her and gave her the news that her son had been killed all 300 of us heard her cries. I don't think I ever witnesses something that intense before in my life. To find out your only son had been killed while you was in prison had to be the worst shit ever. When I tell y'all I can still hear her cries to this day, I can, because she was always making everybody else laugh. It was hard to see her that way. My heart aches just writing this cause even 20 years later I can still feel that pain--still hear those cries of heartache.

I remember they put her on suicidal watch cause she kept saying she had nothing else to live for. It was a very sad time in there. I had gotten so use to the atmosphere I had forgot about the pain of it all. So many people lose their loved ones while locked up and most of the time you are not even allowed to attend the funeral. Annette slept right across from me and I heard every cry. I watched her get up in the middle of the night and just rock back and forth. You could tell she was hurting and there was nothing anybody could do to make it better. Some days I wonder whatever happened to her, like once she got out. Losing your only son and not even being able to put him to rest. How do you even recover after that?

I swear that place gave me a whole different perspective on life. It made me want to do more with my own life. I decided while I was still in Admissions that I was gon make some changes and start trying to be a better me.

I woke up one morning and walked into the dayroom where they let you sign up for all kinda classes and programs. I found a list to get your GED and felt like that was the first thing I should start with. Out of 300 women, only 3 of them wanted to get into the GED program. I was one of the three. I decided from that day on that I was gon get into every program they had just to make my time go by faster. I was gon do my time and not let the time do me. Best decision ever.

Chapter 15

You know what was crazy about me doing my time? None of my so-called best friends held me down. We got all that money together, played niggas together, smoked more weed than the law allowed together, but when it was really time to be down with a mutha fucka I couldn't find nobody. I would've thought that maybe Tonya would at least drop some clothes off to my mom for my shorty but nothing. They just went on like I was at camp or some shit. That shit hurted the most. It's like, Damn, if you can only be there for me during the good times, I don't want you around at all. Prison for sure changed me big time. Like for real, I felt shit happening.

I think maybe I use to judge people without knowing their story. I mean for real, who really cares about what other people have been through right? For instance, you see a crackhead and you assume they wanted to get addicted to crack, right? Wrong. Some people have some really fucked up stories from their childhood. Some people have been in the streets since they were kids so drugs and alcohol came natural to them growing up. I guess I just started looking at people different. I now knew there could be a fucked up story behind any and everybody.

I met a girl in there that was in love with her daddy. Like her real daddy who helped make her. This girl, with long blonde hair, slept next to me so we got to know each other really good. I noticed one day when she was putting on her pajamas that she had a Daddy's girl tat on her tittie. It had a man holding a baby and the baby licking the dad's face. I'm thinking to myself, *That's some weird shit*. We was talking a few days later and she told me that she had a baby by her father. I'm like, whoa. She said her mom was the one that sent her to prison because she was jealous of her. This was some real Jerry Springer shit cause like, where does this even happen at?

Her dad use to send her money and everything and send her cards saying he loves her and can't wait 'til she got out. She told me she had started doing drugs with her mom and dad at the age of 12, and by 15 she was having sex with her dad. I asked her how it even came about and she said they use to be so high they didn't know what they was doing, but ended up falling in love. Then he divorced her mother. Sick as fuck right? She ended up in jail because she was on probation and one day she got really high off some pills and went to confront her mother about some shit she told her aunt. The mother called the police and she was picked up. She said it was all a plot to get back with her daddy. I had never in my mutha fucking life heard of no shit like that. Trust me it was many more of them kinda stories too.

I remember one of my roommates had one of the craziest stories ever. She was serving a 25-to-Life sentence for setting some dude up and her boyfriend killed him. They gave them both 25-to-Life, meaning most likely they were going to die in prison.

She was a real pretty girl—high yellow, long wavy hair like she was mixed with something and a nice lil frame. All the studs in jail wanted her. She told me that when she first got to prison she kept gettting in fights. Everybody probably was trying her cause she was cute.

One night they took her to the hole and that turned out to be the worst night of her bid. The hole is a segregated place you go usually when you get in trouble—sometimes when you outta your mind. She said she was flipping out on everybody and that's why they threw her in. She said she had been in there for about 10 minutes when the sergeant came in—big, tall, black mu-fucka. She said that man raped and beat her for at least 2 hours, and when it was over, threw her in the hole for six months. She hadn't even been there for two months when this happened. Said she almost lost her mind in that one cell for those six months

When they finally let her out, she said she was afraid to tell anybody cause for one, he's the sergeant, what the fuck! And for two, she didn't wanna go back to the hole. She told me I was the first person she had ever told that story to—said she didn't want no smoke.

No matter how much I tried to stick to myself it was like people would always find me to talk. Like, I don't know if I had "Come talk to me" written across my head, but for some strange reason I made those women feel comfortable telling me their stories. I'm so thankful for that now, because now I'm able to share some of them with you. Everything happens for a reason and I needed to go inside so I could change my way of living and thinking. I needed to go to prison because I needed to change my way of seeing people. I knew my life would never be the same after meeting all these women. I knew their stories would be forever embedded in my memories.

One day while I was sitting on my bunk I told my bunky I had decided to write a book called "Soft Women, Hard Time." I don't think I was really serious, but I just thought it was something to do that would help me pass the time. She was the only one I told and I only told her that because she kept asking me to join all kinda activities with her and I just didn't want to be around all those women anymore than I needed to be. I told her that story so she could leave me alone.

Well the total opposite happened. She went and told all her lil friends that I was writing a book about being in jail and before you know it, all kinda women was coming up to me telling me they would be interested in sitting down to tell me their story. After about three different ladies approached me about my book I had to blow down on my bunky. Of course, I found her where she was always hanging out--on the yard with her girlfriend. Yeah, most women who go to prison end up being gay. Well, *Gay for the stay*, is what they call it. You just get a girl to help you pass the time. I definitely was not with that bullshit. I could wait for some dick when I got home.

I walked straight up to my bunky. Her name was Rain. She was serving a Life sentence for not snitching on her boyfriend after he had shot and killed her roomates. Crazy AF right? Yeah, she said her boyfriend had a cameo over her house one night gone off some PCP or something and just flipped out on her and her roomates. She tried to calm him down, but he ended up pulling out a gun and shooting and killing all 3 of her roomates. He fled from the scene and when police came she said she didn't know what happened. They ended up finding out it was him and catching him, but because she never said he did it or what happened, they charged her with the murders too.

Like I said, most women in prison was in there for some shit a man did. I went up to her and asked her why in thee fuck did she tell all these hoes I was doing interviews for my book. Soon as I asked her, both her and her girlfriend started cracking up. They knew I didn't like to even come to the yard, let alone have all these people all in my space.

Rain like "Girl, I told one person and it just spread like wildfire. You gotta understand something," she said. "Most of the people I kick it with is Lifers, just like myself. Most of our stories no one will ever hear because this is our story. We not never leaving this place so our stories will die right here with us. You still got a life to live out there so of course everybody wanna tell you they story. You're our only chance of getting them to the world."

I damn sure wasn't ready for that answer. It had taken me by surprise to be exact. Hit me hard too. She was so right. Here I was, playing, trying to pass time, and these women really had something they wanted to say and they wanted to say it to me. I walked back to the dorm in a stupor. I kept replaying what she had just said to me. Most of these women were never going home. They was going to do all their time and die right here. Shit was sad af for real.

I took a shower and that night I decided I would interview the women who had came up to me. I would not only interview them, but I would make sure their stories didn't just die here in this prison. I would make sure they were heard. I promised myself that. I went to sleep that night full and I hadn't eaten a thing that day. Full of hope, not only for myself, but for those women as well.

The next day I started telling people they could meet with me at different times in the dayroom. The dayroom was a place where you could play games, watch TV, use the phone or anything else that involved socializing. They didn't want other people in your room, so the dayroom was where you could be social at. I turned it into my office. Word got around quick and before you know it I went from the girl who sat in her room to the girl that ran the dayroom, lol. I would sit for hours with these ladies just talking. I was not only learning so much about them, but I was also learning things about myself. I use to think my life and childhood was rough, but I had no idea what so many other women had been through. I swear women are some strong creatures. We can go through hell and manage to still love and produce another life and love them as well. Some of these stories were mind blowing. Like I said before, most of these women had Life sentences, so they were never getting out.

It was scary because most of these stories all had one common theme–a man. I talked with women who were riding with a man not knowing what he was into and before you know it, a shootout occurred. Someone ended up dead and now she was being charged with murder too. I spoke with women whose men used them to set someone up and when things went wrong and someone ended up hurt all the blame went on the women. There were women who had men molesting their daughters and they killed them or tried to kill them, and the women were the ones who ended up in prison–not the men who were committing these horrible crimes. I get chill bumps just thinking about it because for mine, I would do the same. The system is not set up for black people and it's really fucked up for women.

You know what else was messed up? That visiting room. Looks completely different from a men's facility. I've went to visit dudes in jail. It be a waiting list. You be having to sign up weeks in advance. Every day was always available at the women's jail. After all that women did for men, most of them didn't have even do half of their part holding it down while these women were away. A man can do a crime, get Life, and a woman will die doing that bid with him. A woman get 6 months and a nigga be done got a whole new family. It's crazy I swear.

I'm sure there are plenty of judges who know damn well these women had nothing to do with some of these crimes, yet they still charge them as if they did. I'm sitting in prison for boosting and these women in here for shit they didn't even do and they never going home.

I started talking with these women just being nosy and trying to pass the time, but I had become attached to them. It's like every time they told me a story it went straight to my soul and now was renting a place inside of me. The women were beautiful too. Pretty, brownskin, long healthy hair, radiant smiles, and they would live and die here in prison. A lot of people go to prison and learn other ways to commit crimes. I went to prison and learned how to be more understanding. That place changed me like fuck. I will never look at another women and think she's my competition. I don't know what that woman done been through that made her the way she is. I told those women 12 years ago that I was writing a book and 12 yrs later, I'm just getting to it. Life and other things got in the way, but I never forgot them. Never stopped talking about them. Never forgot the stories they told me. Life will take you different places, but you never forget where you been and what you been through. Prison was supposed to break me, but it made it into the woman I am today. I thank God for that.

Chapter 16

While in prison I promised myself I would make some changes once I was released. I didn't know exactly what changes I was going to make, but I just knew going back to prison was completely out of the question. I also made up my mind that I would be an inspiration to those still locked up. I had never before in my whole life met so many women who were hopeless. The system had broken them—made them feel like they weren't shit and would never be shit. People make mistakes and we're all human, but life still goes on. I wanted to show them there was still hope. I wanted to be the reason they believed again.

Upon my release things didn't originally go that way. It was hard trying to do the right thing. To be exact, it was the hardest thing I've ever done. Trying to get a job was the worst. Employers would see that I was just recently released and turn their nose up at my application. I got so tired and discouraged from all the rejection. I kept trying though. My girls were all still doing the same thing and even when I tried to tell them we needed to do something different they just wasn't trying to hear that shit. I found myself trying to be the best version of me all by myself.

It would've been easy to go back to doing what got me in prison in the first place. I wanted more though. Being an entrepreneur was the last thing on my mind. I just kept trying to get a job. I figured somebody was going to give me a chance eventually. Being a boss sorta snuck up on me.

I was riding with one of my long-time friends when her aunt called and asked did she want to be a guest on her new radio show. My girl was like, *Naw,* and hung up. Me being a person who loved to talk I told her I would've loved to be a guest. She looked at me like I was crazy. She was like, *You wanna go on the show?* Uhhh, yeah. I wanted to tell the world about my experiences being locked up and all kinda other shit. She called her back and let me talk to her and by the end of the call I was booked to be a guest on her next show. I was pumped. You would've thought I was about to be on the breakfast club or some shit. I never thought about doing radio before but all of a sudden I was interested. I told everybody I knew to make sure they tuned in to the show. What I didn't know is this station was just starting out and had very few listeners, so they were looking for any action they could get.

When the day came for me to go on I was ready. I had written down all type of things I wanted to talk about and even questions I wanted to ask the host. Soon as I touched that mic something clicked in my soul. I swear I was a natural. All my people was tuned in and calling in. The host of the show was impressed. They told me that they had never had that many listeners and callers ever. They like, *Girl who is you?* I'm thinking to myself, nobody for real. We had a great show with some really dope conversations. It went so well they asked me to come back again the following week. I felt like a star leaving and it felt really good inside. It was crazy because out of all the people that had tuned in none of my girls did. That shit hurt. I felt like, Damn, I'm trying to do something different and the least they could've done was tune in. They say when you start doing right and finding yourself you lose a lot of people on the way. They wasn't never lying. I didn't trip though, I just held my head up high and started preparing for next week's show.

The next show was even better than the first. I had told even more people about it and everybody tuned in. When I talked to the people that listened to the first show they told me that they loved hearing me coming through their speakers. They also said they didn't really care to hear everybody else though. That had me thinking that maybe I needed my own show. I knew I hadn't went to any broadcasting school or anything, but it felt so natural to me. I didn't think I was ready yet though.

Show number 2 was a hit as well and after the show the host told me they wanted to have a talk with me. They asked me to be a permanent host on their show. I was beyond flattered. I was thinking like, *Wow, they wanted me, this lil brownskin hood chick who was just recently let out of prison be a permanent host on their show?* Before I agreed to it I asked them what it would take for me to have my own show. The looks in their eyes told me they were not feeling my idea. They started telling me that I wasn't ready for my own show and that even though I did good it would take a lot of hard work and dedication and they didn't think I was up for the job. I don't know about anybody else, but when someone tells me I can't do something that makes me wanna show them I can. I didn't even want to be on their show anymore. I wanted to prove to them I could do my own and do it well.

They gave me a million reasons why I shouldn't, but I was determined and it wasn't anything they could do to change my mind. They told me they would think about it and let me know.

I went home that night and planned out my whole show from the title to segments. I wanted to do a morning show. I wanted to wake people up with some motivation every morning. Some thug motivation at that. I wanted to be fully prepared so when I spoke with them again they would see how serious I was. I named my show *Wake and Bake*. Even though I was trying to do things the right way I still hadn't stopped smoking weed. That shit was the healer to all of my problems— well at least I thought it was. I also thought of a bunch of different segments I would have on my show and the best segment in my eyes was "Free My Nigga Friday," which would be dedicated to all of the men and women locked up behind bars. I wanted to remind people in the free world that they needed to not forget about their families that was in jail. It's so easy to say fuck em when they outta site outta mind. I also wanted to be the voice for them. I wanted to show the world that even though I had a past, that did not determine my future. People give cheaters second chances all the time, so why couldn't felons get a second chance? I felt like this was my second chance and I wasn't going to fuck this up. It was my time to prove not only to the world, but also to myself that I was more than just a booster from EC. I had dreams and goals too and just because I been to prison that wasn't going to stop me from going after them.

I eventually got a call from the owner and the host and they said they might've been willing to give me a chance, but I would have to show them a summary of what my show would consist of. I smiled when they said that because they had no idea I already did that. I reached in my bag and pulled out my completed outline of Wake and Bake. It had the title of the show, the times I wanted to come on, and segments for every day of the week. I wanted my show to be a daily morning show Monday thru Friday from 9-10 am. Needless to say they were impressed. They could not believe I had already done what they wanted me to do. I guess they finally realized how serious I was. So yeah I got my own show and it was a big hit.

I had guest on my show who are now doing amazing things but they had their first interview with me. I went from 9-10am, to 9-noon after just 30 days. The people wanted to hear more of me so my show got extended. For the first time in my life I felt so good about myself. I didn't even realize the impact I was having on people. I just wanted to talk my talk.

I started seeing people out in my city and they started telling me how inspiring I was and to keep up the good work. I was shocked. I had never before been called inspiring. I been called a hoe and a thief and all kinda other things, but being called inspiring was new to me and I liked it. Honestly, at first when I got on the radio I was just trying to be entertaining, but after I realized so many people were listening I started making sure I really had something to talk about. After people started telling me I was inspiring them I made sure to constantly give them some inspiration and by doing that all I did was tell my own story.

In my community, it wasn't normal to be chasing your goals. A lot of people I grew up with was still in the hood doing the same shit we were doing as kids. That's why so many of your own people don't support you. It's not what they're use to and people hate change. I still wasn't fully in my purpose, but I was getting there. You have to really want to change in order for God to start aligning you with your true purpose. I did radio for 6 years before I truly changed but every year I got better. Every obstacle I got through there was a lesson to be learned.

Let me tell y'all this, running my business and trying to do right was one of the hardest things to do. I'm not gone even tell y'all how many men I've worked with that have disrespected me. Men hate a woman in control, even if you don't treat them like you're in control. I took it all on the chin though and did it with a smile on my face. I chose not to speak on all the fuck shit that happened during the beginning stages of my radio career. It is what it is. The best part about it all is that I learned from it. I didn't let any of it stop me from moving forward. Yeah, it may have knocked me off my block a few times but I always got back up.

Somewhere around 6 years into my radio career I started to feel empty. I began feeling like somewhere down this crazy road I got sidetracked. I noticed my shows had stopped being inspiring and started being about a bunch of bullshit. I didn't know how it got to this, but I didn't like it. I started digging deep inside myself and asking why did I start this journey. Was it to entertain or was it to inspire? My whole plan for even doing radio was to be a voice for people like me—people who have been incarcerated and people who have been counted out. Free My Nigga Friday had turned into Freaky Friday and I didn't even know how that happened—well, yes I do. I started trying to please the world. The world didn't really want to hear about people that was locked up. They don't care, so I changed it to Freak Friday because people always wanted to talk about sex. I was losing myself and my vision and I didn't like the way I was feeling. I even voiced my concern to my listeners. I was crying out for help, but no one really payed attention or they just really didn't care.

I got so fed up that I just stopped. Just ended my show with no warning or no explanation. I felt empty and I refused to go on and push my emptiness out into the world. People thought I was crazy and kept asking me what happened to the show. I didn't give a fuck because at that point I needed to find my why. Why I started in the first place and where I wanted to go. Where I wanted my career to go. I needed to take some time to find myself.

I think people be afraid to admit that they're lost or afraid to admit they don't have any direction. I wasn't. I was gon take some time to find me for me. Let's just say that was the best thing I ever did.

I started traveling more and along the way I started meeting other people who had been to prison and was doing some amazing things. I couldn't believe it. On everything, it was like God was sending me on a mission to meet these people. In the middle of me feeling like I was losing myself God was showing me the way. All of a sudden I started realizing what my purpose was. People talked so much mess about me having felonies and going to prison, but truth is, there was so much inspiration in my story. I didn't let my past circumstances hold me back. Yes I was a felon, but I was doing more positive shit than mu-fuckas who had a clean record.

In the process of me finding myself I met a woman from New York by the name of Jamila T. Davis. I had interviewed her on my radio show and I continued to follow her story via social media. She had just gotten out of jail from serving a 12-year sentence, but she was doing some amazing things in her community. I was very impressed by how she was moving and also very inspired. We became quite close and one day she told me to get from behind that mic and get out into the community. She said the world needs to hear your voice, BUT they also need to see your face. Not really sure if she even knew that that conversation changed my whole attitude. From that one conversation I created *Stoney in the City*. I wanted to get out into the world and meet more dope people like Jamila and myself. I wanted to highlight people with a past that was doing some amazing things worldwide. I took my show on the road too. That's where my inspiration came from. I started meeting so many people with crazy stories wayyy worse than mine, but they were making big moves. They were inspiring people and showing the world that you couldn't count us out just because we had a past.

Finding your true purpose feels like you've made it to heaven or at least that's how it made me feel. When you start moving a certain kinda way God will start opening more doors for you. I started speaking out about the injustice of inmates and standing up for people in my community, I started truly being the voice for my people and it was all from the heart. You know what else happened during this process? I started weeding out the people in my life that didn't belong. It's crazy because I didn't have to do much because just being positive makes people wanna distance themselves. A lot of people don't wanna change. They wanna continue doing what they've always done so trying to do better takes too much out of them I guess. At that point I didn't give a fuck who I lost as long as I didn't lose myself again. The more people I lost the more I started meeting really dope people with really great spirits. A lot of these people didn't have a felony background, but they all believed in change. They also saw my vision and not only believed in it, but believed in me. Something amazing was happening and I was loving every minute of it. That's when I started writing this book.

I first started on this book years ago when I was on house arrest for catching a boosting case, but as soon as I got off I ain't think shit else about it. I would go back every now and then, but I could never really focus cause I was always in a different state of mind each time I revisited it. This time around I started it all over. I was in full purpose mode and I needed to get this story out. It was something that I started that I was ready to finish and put out into the world. I wrote this book to show people how you cannot let your past hinder you from having an amazing future. I wrote this book to show the world that I'm far from perfect, but my heart is as pure as it gets and I was meant to inspire others. If I would've let some of those obstacles stop me I would not be here today to tell y'all these stories. When you go to prison society wants you to believe that you will never be shit—that you will never amount to anything—that your life is pretty much over. Well I'm here to tell you and show you different.

I have 3 felonies on my record, but I'm also a business owner, a great mom, and the founder of my non-profit called *Inmate2inspiration,* designed to help people transition back into the free world after being released from prison. I'm also an activist, a Prison Reform advocate and now I'm an author too, yayyyyyy. What I didn't know was that the more I stand up and speak about Prison Reform the more I realize it's all politics. Like, everything always comes back to politics. I'm thinking I might just be the mayor of East Cleveland. Maybe, I don't know.

None of this journey was easy, but it was all worth it. I hope I inspire more people with a past to go after their dreams. Hell if you don't have a past I still wish to inspire you as well. Nothing comes to a sleeper but a good night's rest. We all have a story to tell so make sure its a good one. Like another good friend of mine who created *Comma Club* clothing while doing a 15-year sentence for something he didn't do. He says, "His Story Ain't Over." Now a free man after being exonerated, he's showing the world just like that. No matter what life has thrown at you, no matter how many people don't believe in you, it's truly up to you to dig deep down inside of yourself and find the inspiration you truly need. I hope my story can help one person out there that's feeling like it's over. It ain't never over. My past pushed me to my purpose and I love it here!!!

Made in the USA
Columbia, SC
05 June 2021